THE ON...

"A fierce and dama[ged]... [fi]erce and damaged people—and children, and animals—with a brilliant, painful innocence that has no equal in literature. He is so good at hurt and shame—how did he also manage to be so funny? I have laughed at his great Arthurian novel and cried over it and loved it all my life."

—Ursula K. Le Guin

"Certain books offer pleasures so rich and enduring, they become part of what defines us. *The Once and Future King* is like that for me. It manages—by some miracle—to be about its own time, and a distant, legendary time, and about today. It mingles wisdom, wonderful, laugh-out-loud humor, and deep sorrow—while telling one of the great tales of the Western world. I envy the reader coming to it for the first time."

—Guy Gavriel Kay

"I have read [this] book more times than any other in my library ... White took hold of the ultimate English epic and recast it in modern literary language, sacrificing none of its grandeur or its strangeness in the process, and adding in all the humor and passion that we expect from a novel. What was once as stiff and two-dimensional as a medieval tapestry becomes rich and real and devastatingly sad."

—Lev Grossman

"Touching, profound, funny, and tragic."

—*Los Angeles Times*

"Richly imagined and unfailingly eloquent and entertaining, its appeal is timeless and universal. If a reader reads only one Arthurian tale, let this be it."

—*Booklist*

continued . . .

"*The Once and Future King* is full of insights, scenes, and flourishes that are really quite astonishing."
—*The Guardian* (UK)

"A gay, warm, sad, glinting, rich, mystical, true, and beautiful tapestry of human history and human spirit."
—*Minneapolis Tribune*

"Woven together with literary genius, archeological authority, and a freshness which is as bright as the dawn and the memories we associated with a golden age. It is hard to say at which level White's greatness is most special."
—*The Christian Science Monitor*

"Ambitious . . . It will long remain a memorial to an author who is at once civilized, learned, witty, and humane."
—*The Times Literary Supplement*

"*The Once and Future King* is a once and future book . . . Shows every sign of staying a classic."
—*New York World-Telegram*

"Will become without a doubt one of the classics of English literature." —*American Statesman*

"An extraordinary achievement . . . [White's] success is due to a happy blend of imagination, scholarly research, psychological insight, and humor."
—*Humanities Association Bulletin*

"Intensely contemporary and pungent . . . Not only better . . . and richer for being a retelling, it is also more original. In fact, there is everything in this great book."
—*Saturday Review*

"Should be enormously popular and become one of the curious classics of English literature." —David Garnett

THE BOOK OF MERLYN
The Unpublished Conclusion to
The Once and Future King

T. H. WHITE

Prologue by Sylvia Townsend Warner
Illustrations by Trevor Stubley

ACE BOOKS, NEW YORK

THE BERKLEY PUBLISHING GROUP
Published by the Penguin Group
Penguin Group (USA) LLC
375 Hudson Street, New York, New York 10014

USA • Canada • UK • Ireland • Australia • New Zealand • India • South Africa • China

penguin.com

A Penguin Random House Company

THE BOOK OF MERLYN

An Ace Book / published by arrangement with University of Texas Press

Ace Books are published by The Berkley Publishing Group.
ACE and the "A" design are trademarks of Penguin Group (USA) LLC.

For information, address: University of Texas Press,
P.O. Box 7819, Austin, Texas 78713.

ISBN: 978-0-441-07015-2

PUBLISHING HISTORY
University of Texas Press edition / 1977
Berkley edition / September 1978
Ace mass-market edition / September 1987

PRINTED IN THE UNITED STATES OF AMERICA

33 32 31 30 29 28 27 26 25 24

Cover art by Christian Dente.
Cover design by Erika Fusari.

The original manuscript of *The Book of Merlyn* is in the T. H. White
Collection, Humanities Research Center, The University of Texas at Austin.

Pages 66–72 and 101–126 of *The Book of Merlyn* have appeared, in slightly
modified form, in *The Once and Future King*, copyright 1939, 1940 by T. H. White,
© 1958 by T. H. White and published by G. P. Putnam's Sons, pages 122–130 and
164–177. The same pages have also appeared in the original British edition of
The Once and Future King, published by William Collins' Sons & Co.

Publisher's Statement

The Book of Merlyn, written by T. H. White
during World War II, was intended to be the
concluding book of a planned five-book volume
entitled *The Once and Future King*. While *The
Once and Future King* was indeed finally
published in 1958, *The Book of Merlyn* was not
included. This is the first time it has ever fully
appeared in print.

White did not see proofs of *The Book of
Merlyn* after the complete manuscript was
submitted for publication late in 1941, and, as he
was in the habit of making corrections and
revisions once his work was set in type, this
manuscript was not in final form when it came to
us. However, it seemed to be so nearly finished
that only minimal editing was necessary.

The 1958 Putnam edition of *The Once and
Future King* was used as a guide in our editing.
The use of punctuation in dialogue was

regularized. All errors in spelling were corrected, and British and archaic spellings were retained. Book titles and, usually, genus/species names were italicized, and, where White had been inconsistent in capitalizing such words as badger, man, and democracy, capitalization was regularized. In a few cases, where the typist had obviously omitted a word, that word has been inserted.

Two episodes in *The Book of Merlyn*—scenes where Merlyn transforms Arthur into an ant and later into a goose—have already appeared somewhat out of context in *The Sword in the Stone* as published in the tetralogy. White had originally written them for *The Book of Merlyn* in his five-book version of *The Once and Future King*, and we have therefore let them stand.

Where Latin or Greek is not translated in the original manuscript, a translation has kindly been provided by Peter Green.

THE BOOK OF MERLYN
The Unpublished Conclusion to
The Once and Future King

1

The Story of the Book

> *The dream, like the one before it, lasted about
> half an hour. In the last three minutes of the
> dream some fishes, dragons and such-like ran
> hurriedly about. A dragon swallowed one of the
> pebbles, but spat it out.*
>
> *In the ultimate twinkling of an eye, far tinier in
> time than the last millimetre on a six-foot rule,
> there came a man. He split up the one pebble
> which remained of all that mountain with blows;
> then made an arrow-head of it, and slew his
> brother.*
>
> The Sword in the Stone
> *Chapter 18, original version*

"MY FATHER made me a wooden castle big enough
to get into, and he fixed real pistol barrels beneath
its battlements to fire a salute on my birthday, but
made me sit in front the first night—that deep

Indian night—to receive the salute, and I,
believing I was to be shot, cried."

Throughout his life White was subject to fears:
fears from without—a menacing psychopathic
mother, the prefects at Cheltenham College
"rattling their canes," poverty, tuberculosis, public
opinion; fears from within—fear of being afraid,
of being a failure, of being trapped. He was afraid
of death, afraid of the dark. He was afraid of his
own proclivities, which might be called vices:
drink, boys, a latent sadism. Notably free from
fearing God, he was basically afraid of the human
race. His life was a running battle with these fears,
which he fought with courage, levity, sardonic wit,
and industry. He was never without a project,
never tired of learning, and had a high opinion of
his capacities.

This high opinion was shared by his teachers at
the University of Cambridge. When tuberculosis
tripped him in his second year, a group of dons
made up a sum of money sufficient to send him to
Italy for a year's convalescence. He took to Italy
like a duck to water, learned the language, made
some low friends, studied pension life, and wrote
his first novel, *They Winter Abroad*. The
inaugurator of the convalescent fund recalled:
"... he returned in great form, determined to have
the examiner's blood in Part II; and sure enough
in 1929 he took a tearing First Class with
Distinction."

In 1932, on a Cambridge recommendation, he
was appointed head of the English Department at
Stowe School.

It was a position of authority under an

enlightened headmaster who allowed him ample
rope. His pupils still remember him, some for the
stimulus of his teaching, others for the sting of his
criticism, others again for extracurriculum
rambles in search of grass snakes. He learned to
fly, in order to come to terms with a fear of falling
from high places, and to think rather better of the
human race by meeting farm laborers at the local
inn. After a couple of years he tired of Stowe, and
decided on no evidence that his headmaster meant
to get rid of him. With poverty a fear to be
reckoned with, he constructed two potboilers and
compiled another. An Easter holiday fishing in
rain and solitude on a Highland river showed him
what he really wanted—to write in freedom, to
land a book of his own as well as a salmon.

At midsummer 1936 he gave up his post and
rented a gamekeeper's cottage at Stowe Ridings
on the Stowe estate. The compiled potboiler, made
up of extracts from his fishing, hunting, shooting,
and flying diaries and called *England Have My
Bones,* sold so well that its publisher undertook to
pay him £200 a year against a yearly book.

The gamekeeper's cottage stood among
woodlands—a sturdy Victorian structure without
amenities. It was by lamplight that White pulled
from a shelf the copy of the *Morte d'Arthur* he
had used for the essay on Malory he submitted for
the English tripos, Part I. Then he had been
concerned with the impression he would make on
the examiners. Now he read with a free mind.

One of the advantages of having taken a First
Class with Distinction in English is a capacity to
read. White read the *Morte d'Arthur* as acutely as

though he were reading a brief. The note in which he summarized his findings may be his first step toward *The Once and Future King:*

"The whole Arthurian story is a regular greek doom, comparable to that of Orestes.

"Uther started the wrong-doing upon the family of the duke of Cornwall, and it was the descendant of that family who finally revenged the wrong upon Arthur. The fathers have eaten sour grapes etc. Arthur had to pay for his father's initial transgression, but, to make it fairer, the fates ordained that he himself should also make a transgression (against the Cornwalls) in order to bind him more closely in identification with the doom.

"It happened like this.

"The Duke of Cornwall married Igraine and they had three daughters, Morgan le Fay, Elaine and Morgause.

"Uther Pendragon fell in love with Igraine and slew her husband in war, in order to get her. Upon her he begot Arthur, so that Arthur was half brother to the three girls. But he was brought up separately.

"The girls married Uriens, Nentres and Lot, all kings. They would naturally have a dislike for Uther and anybody who had anything to do with Uther.

"When Uther died and Arthur succeeded him in mysterious circumstances, naturally Arthur inherited this feud. The girls persuaded their husbands to lead a revolt of eleven kings.

"Arthur had been told that Uther was his father, but Uther had been a vigourous old gentleman and Merlyn had very stupidly forgotten to tell Arthur who his mother was.

"After a great battle in which the 11 kings were subdued, Morgause, the wife of King Lot, came to Arthur on an embassy. They did not know of their relationship at this time. They fell for each other, went to bed together, and the result was *Mordred*. Mordred was thus the fruit of incest (his father was his mother's half brother), and it was he who finally brought the doom on Arthur's head. The sin was incest, the punishment Guinever, and the instrument of punishment Mordred, the fruit of the sin. It was Mordred who insisted on blowing the gaff on Launcelot and Guinever's affair, which Arthur was content to overlook, so long as it was not put into words."

En trentiesme année de mon aage
Quand toutes mes hontes j'ai bues

White was thirty when he rented the gamekeeper's cottage. He had done with his past, he was on good terms with himself, he was free. His solitude was peopled by a succession of hawks, a rescued tawny owl, a setter bitch on whom he unloosed his frustrated capacity to love. Now in the *Morte d'Arthur,* he had a subject into which he could unloose his frustrated capacity for hero worship, his accumulated miscellany of scholarship, his love of living, his admiration of Malory. It is as though, beginning a new subject, he wrote as a novice. Instead of the arid dexterity of the potboilers, *The Sword in the Stone* has the impetus and recklessness of a beginner's work. It is full of poetry, farce, invention, iconoclasm, and, above all, the reverence due to youth in its portrayal of the young Arthur. It was accepted for publication on both sides of the Atlantic, and in the United States was being considered by the Book of the Month Club—who took it. But it was 1938, the year of Munich; the pistol barrels in the toy fort were charged for more than a salute. Fear of war half choked him when he was fitted with a gasmask, retreated when Chamberlain bought peace on Hitler's terms, but could not be dismissed.

White's thinking was typical of the postwar epoch. War was a ruinous dementia. It silenced law, it killed poets, it exalted the proud, filled the greedy with good things, and oppressed the humble and meek; no good could come of it, it was hopelessly out of date. No one wanted it. (Unfortunately, no one had passionately wanted the League of Nations, either.) If, against reason and common sense, another war should break out, he must declare himself a conscientious objector. In the first lemming rush to volunteer, he wrote to David Garnett: "I have written to Siegfried Sassoon and the headmaster of Stowe (my poor list of influential people) to ask them if they can get me any sensible job in this wretched war, if it starts. This is the ultimatum: I propose to enlist as a private soldier in one month after the outbreak of hostilities, unless one of you gets me an *efficient* job before that."

Chamberlain capitulated, the crisis went off the boil, White began *The Witch in the Wood* (the second volume of *The Once and Future King*) and was diverted to *Grief for the Grey Geese,* a novel he never finished. It was conceived in a state of intense physical excitement. He was alone, he was in the intimidating sea-level territory of the Wash, he was pursuing a long-ambitioned desire, intricately compounded of sporting prowess and sadism—to shoot a wild goose in flight. The theme is significant. The geese are warred on by the goose shooters. Among the goose shooters is a renegade who takes sides with the geese, deflecting their flight away from the ranks of the shooters. White plainly identifies himself with the renegade, while bent on shooting a wild goose.

In January 1939 he wrote to Garnett, who had invited him to go salmon fishing in Ireland: "If only I can get out of this doomed country before the crash, I shall be happy. Two years of worry on the subject have convinced me that I had better run for my life, and have a certain right to do so. I may just as well do this as shoot myself on the outbreak of hostilities. I don't like war, I don't want war, and I didn't start it. I think I could just bear life as a coward, but I couldn't bear it as a hero."

A month later he was in Ireland, lodging in a farmhouse called Doolistown, in County Meath, where he proposed to stay long enough to finish *The Witch in the Wood* (published shortly thereafter) and catch a salmon. It was his home for the next six and a half years. For six of them he never heard an English voice and rarely a cultivated one. Provincial Ireland swallowed him like a deep bog.

He had escaped his doomed country, but he could not avoid being in earshot of it.

Diary, April 26th, 1939
Conscription is now seriously spoken of in England, and everybody lives from one speech of Hitler's to the next. I read back in this book at the various tawdry little decisions which I have tried to make under the pressure of the Beast: to be a conscientious objector, and then to fight, and then to seek some constructive wartime employment which might combine creative work with service to my country. All these sad and terrified dashes from one hunted corner to the next.

Meanwhile he tried to protect his peace of mind by dashes in new directions. Lodging in a Catholic household and treated as one of the family, he considered becoming a Catholic. Because his father had happened to be born in Ireland, he deluded himself with an idea of Irish ancestry. He read books on Irish history, with scholarly dispassionateness reading authors on either side of that vexed question; he tried to learn Erse, going once a week to the local schoolmaster for lessons and "doing an hour's prep every morning"; he looked for a habitation, and rented a house called Sheskin Lodge in County Mayo for the shooting; later, he made researches into the legendary Godstone on the island of Inniskea. More to the purpose, being involuntary, he was captured by the somber beauty, the desolate charm, of Erris—that part of County Mayo lying between the Nephin Beg range and the sea.

It was at Sheskin Lodge, embowered in fuchsias and rhododrendron thickets and surrounded by leagues of bog, that he heard the last English voices. They were saying Goodbye. War had been declared, the visiting Garnetts were going back to England.

The tenancy of Sheskin ran out, he returned to Doolistown and listened to the news.

October 20th, 1939
There don't seem to be many people being killed yet—no hideous slaughters of gas and bacteria.
But the truth is going.
We are suffocating in propaganda instead of gas, slowly feeling our minds go dead.

October 23rd
The war as one hears of it over the wireless is more terrible than anything I can imagine of mere death. It seems to me that death must be a noble and terrible mystery, whatever one's creed or one's circumstances of dying. It is a natural thing, anyway. But what is happening over the wireless is not natural. The timbre of the voices which sing about Hitler and death is a sneering, nasal mock-timbre. Devils in hell must sing like this.

By then he was preparing for *The Ill-Made Knight* (*The Witch in the Wood,* delivered to his publisher six months earlier, had been returned with a request that it might be rewritten) and making an analysis of the character of Malory's Sir Lancelot—with traits akin to his own:

"Probably sadistic, or he would not have taken such frightful care to be gentle.... Fond of being alone."

In the analysis of Guenever, where he had nothing personal to go on, he speculates, and does his best to overcome his aversion to women. "Guenever had some good characteristics. She chose the best lover she could have done and was brave enough to let him be her lover." "Guenever hardly seems to have been a favourite of Malory's, whatever Tennyson may have thought about her."

It was a new departure for White to approach a book so deliberately or write it so compactly. There is no easy-going writing in *The Ill-Made Knight,* where the Doom tightens on Arthur, and Lancelot is compelled to be instrumental in it by his love for Guenever.

He wrote it in Erris, in the small-town hotel at Belmullet, between researches into the Godstone, lying out on freezing mornings waiting for the passage of the wild geese, local jovialities, and drinking fits after which he would lock himself in his hotel bedroom in terror of the I.R.A.

On October 1st, having completed *The Ill-Made Knight,* he put Erris behind him and went back to Doolistown to write *The Candle in the Wind.* This, the last *Morte d'Arthur* book, in which the doomed king staggers from defeat to defeat, already existed as the skeleton of a play. White was incapable of writing slowly. By midautumn the play was brought to life as a narrative, and he was considering titles for the complete tetralogy: The Ancient Wrong... Arthur Pendragon...

November 14th, 1940

Pendragon can still be saved, and elevated into a superb success, by altering the last part of Book 4, and taking Arthur back to his animals. The legend of his going underground at the end, into the badger's sett, where badger, hedgehog, snake, pike (stuffed in case) and all the rest of them can be waiting to talk it over with him. Now, with Merlyn, they must discuss war from the naturalist's point of view, as I have been doing in this diary lately. They must decide to talk thoroughly over, during Arthur's long retirement underground, the relation of Man to the other animals, in the hope of getting a new angle on his problem from this. Such, indeed, was Merlyn's original objective in introducing him to the animals in the first place. Now what can we learn about abolition of war from animals?

Pendragon can still be saved. Another salvation was involved.

White had gone to Belmullet assuming himself to be at home in Ireland. He came away an Englishman in exile. He had been received, and welcomed as something new to talk about; he had never been accepted. Another Ancient Wrong forbade it—the cleft between the hated and the hating race. He was believed to be a spy (the rumour of an English invasion had kept most of Belmullet sitting up all night); his movements were watched; he was reported to the police and not allowed to leave the mainland; he had joined the local security force, but was asked not to attend parades. His disillusionment may have been rubbed in by the parallel with *The Candle in the Wind,* where Arthur's goodwill is of no avail against his hereditary enemies. Now another winter lay before him, a winter of intellectual loneliness, with only himself to consult, only himself to feed on. He had a roof over his head, a room to be alone in, regular meals, the hedged landscape of County Meath to walk his dog in, nothing much to complain of, nothing to go on with. War had imprisoned him in a padded cell.

It was his own salvation he leaped at.

On December 6th, he wrote to L. J. Potts, formerly his tutor at Cambridge, continuously his Father Confessor in Letters: "The next volume is to be called The Candle in the Wind (one has to add D.V. nowadays)...It will end on the night before the last battle, with Arthur absolutely wretched. And after that I am going to add a new 5th volume, in which Arthur rejoins Merlyn underground (it turns out to be the badger's sett of Vol. I) and the animals come back again, mainly ants and wild geese. Don't squirm. The inspiration is godsent. You see, I have suddenly discovered that (1) the central theme of Morte d'Arthur is to find an antidote to war, (2) that the best way to examine the politics of man is to observe him, with Aristotle, as a political animal. I don't want to go into all this now, it will spoil the freshness of the future book, but I have been thinking a great deal, in a Sam Butlerish way, about man as an animal among animals—his cerebrum, etc. I think I can really make a comment on all these futile isms (communism, fascism, conservatism, etc.) by stepping back—

right back into the real world, in which man is only one of the innumerable other animals. So to put my 'moral' across (but I shan't state it), I shall have the marvellous opportunity of bringing the wheel full circle, and ending on an animal note like the one I began on. This will turn my completed epic into a perfect fruit, 'rounded off and bright and done.'"

On the same day he wrote to Garnett, asking what book it was in which Garnett alleged having read that Malory raided a convent, and continuing, "So far as I can see, my fifth volume is going to be all about the anatomy of the brain. It sounds odd for Arthur, but it is true. Do you happen to know, offhand, of a pretty elementary but efficient book about brain anatomy in *animals, fish, insects, etc.?* I want to know what sort of cerebellum an ant has, also a wild goose. You are the sort of person who would know this."

Though White uses the future tense in his letters to Potts, it is unlikely that he waited from November 14th to December 6th before beginning *The Book of Merlyn*. Book 5, taking up where the original Book 4 ended, has an immediacy of plain statement that could not have brooked much delay. Arthur is still sitting alone in his tent at Salisbury, awaiting his last battle in the final insolvency of his hopes, and weeping the slow tears of old age. When Merlyn enters to renew their former master-pupil relationship and sees the extent of Arthur's misery, he is not sure whether he can do so at this late hour. His assurance that legend will perpetuate Arthur and the Round Table long after history has mislaid them falls on inattentive ears. He invokes their past relationship. The pupil has outgrown the master and puts him off with a *Le roy s'advisera.* Nowhere in the four previous volumes had White made Arthur so much a king as in this portrayal of him defeated. In *Farewell Victoria,* his novel of the early thirties, he hit on the phrase "the immortal generals of defeat." In the first chapter of *The Book of Merlyn* he substantiated it.

But the scheme of Book 5 is to take Arthur underground, where the animals of Book 1 are waiting to talk to him, and where Merlyn is to subject him to the contents of White's notebook so that he may discover what can be learned from animals about the abolition of war.

Since animals avoid warring with their kind, this could be a good subject to examine.

But the discussion is slanted from the first by Merlyn's insistence on the inferiority of man. *Liber scriptus proferetur* ... Merlyn has opened White's notebook, and finds small evidence that man deserves to be placed among the two thousand eight hundred and fifty species of mammalian animals in the world. They know how to behave befittingly, existing without war or usurpation. Man does not. Merlyn weakens the denunciation by adding the insult that man is a parvenu.

At this point no one present is impious enough to suggest that man may do better in time.

At a later stage of the discussion Arthur, the representative of the parvenu species, suggests that man has had a few good ideas, such as buildings and arable fields. He is put in his place by the achievements of coral animals, beavers, seed-carrying birds, and finally felled with the earthworm, so much esteemed by Darwin. The distinction between performing and planned performance is not allowed to occur to him, and the conversation sweeps on to nomenclature: *Homo ferox* (*sapiens* being out of the question), *Homo stultus, Homo impoliticus*. The last is the most damning; man must remain savage and dunderheaded till, like the other mammalian species, he learns to live peaceably.

It is easy to pick holes in White's rhetoric. *The Book of Merlyn* was written with the improvidence of an impulse. It holds much that is acute, disturbing, arresting, much that is brilliant, much that is moving, besides a quantity of information. But Merlyn, the main speaker, is made a mouthpiece for spleen, and the spleen is White's. His fear of the human race, which he seemed to have got the better of, had recurred, and was intensified into fury, fury against the human race, who make war and glorify it.

No jet of spleen falls on the figure of Arthur. Whenever he emerges from the torrent of instruction, he is a good character: slow to anger, willing to learn, and no fool. He is as recuperable as grass, and enjoys listening to so much good talk. When Merlyn tells him that to continue his education he must become an ant, he is ready and willing. Magicked into an ant, he enters the ants' nest which Merlyn keeps for scientific purposes. What he sees there is White's evocation of the totalitarian state. Compelled by his outward form to function as a working ant, he is so outraged by the slavish belligerence and futility of his fellow workers that he opposes an ant army in full march, and has to be snatched away by Merlyn.

For his last lesson White consigns him to what by then must have seemed an irrecoverable happiness: the winter of 1938 when he went goose shooting.

It is an insight into how many experiences White packed into his days and how vividly he experienced them that little more than two years had elapsed between *Grief for the Grey Geese* and *The Book of Merlyn*. He had taken the goose book with him when he went to fish in Ireland, and Chapter 12 of *The Book of Merlyn* opens with its description of the dimensionless dark flatness of the Lincolnshire Wash and the horizontal wind blowing over it. But now it is Arthur, become a goose, who faces the wind and feels the slob under his webbed feet, though he is not completely a goose as he has yet to fly. When the flock gathers and takes off for the dawn flight, he rises with it.

The old patch shames the new garment. In that winter of two years before, White was at the height of himself, braced against an actual experience, his senses alert, his imagination flaring like a bonfire in the wind. "I am so physically healthy," he wrote to Sydney Cockerell, "that I am simply distended with sea-air and icebergs and dawn and dark and sunset, so hungry and sober and wealthy and wise, that my mind has gone quite to sleep."

At Doolistown his mind was insomniac, vexed, and demanding. It allowed him to extend the vitality of the old patch over the few pages where

Arthur watches the geese. But with Chapter 13 the intention to convince drives out the creative intention to state, and with but one intermission— when the hedgehog leads Arthur to a hill in the west-country, where he sits looking at his sleeping kingdom under the moon and is reconciled to the bad because of the good—the book clatters on like a factory with analysis, proof and counterproof, exhortation, demonstration, explanation, historical examples, parables from nature—even the hedgehog talks too much.

Yet the theme was good, and timely, and heartfelt, and White preserves an awareness of persons and aerates the dialectics with traits of character and colloquial asides. It is clear from the typescript that he recognized the need for this, for many of these mitigations were added by hand. Whenever he can escape from his purpose— no less aesthetically fell for being laudable—into his rightful kingdom of narrative, *The Book of Merlyn* shows him still master of his peculiar powers. It is as though the book were written by two people: the storyteller and the clever man with the notebook who shouts him down.

Perhaps he went astray in that stony desert of words and opinions because he lacked his former guide. In the final chapter, Malory has returned. Under his tutelage White tells how, after Arthur's death in battle, Guenever and Lancelot, stately abbess and humble hermit, came to their quiet ends. These few pages are among the finest that White ever wrote. Cleverness and contention and animus are dismissed: there is no place for them in the completed world of legend, where White and

Malory stand farewelling at the end of the long journey that began by lamplight in the gamekeeper's cottage at Stowe Ridings.

This is the true last chapter of *The Once and Future King,* and should have its place there. Fate saw otherwise. "I have suddenly discovered that ... the central theme of Morte d'Arthur is to find an antidote to war." To give weight to his discovery by making it seem less sudden, White incorporated new material into the already published three volumes. In November 1941 he sent them, together with *The Candle in the Wind* and *The Book of Merlyn,* to his London publisher, to be published as a whole. Mr. Collins was disconcerted. He replied that the proposal would need thinking over. So long a book would take a great deal of paper. The prosecution of war made heavy demands on the paper supply: forms in triplicate, regulations, reports, instructions to civilians, light reading for forces, etc. White insisted that the five books should appear as a whole. After prolonged negotiations, in the course of which White's demand to see *The Book of Merlyn* in proof escaped notice—a grave pity, for he was accustomed to rely on print to show up what was faulty or superfluous—the fivefold *Once and Future King* was laid by.

The Once and Future King was not published till 1958. It was published as a tetralogy. *The Book of Merlyn,* that attempt to find an antidote to war, had become a war casualty.

Sylvia Townsend Warner

Introducing The Book of Merlyn

WE NOW FIND King Arthur of England, sitting in his campaign tent on the eve of battle. Tomorrow, he will face his bastard son Mordred and that youth's army of Nazi-like Thrashers on the battlefield.

His reign has been painfully long for Arthur, and he is bent with age and sadness and defeat. After a happy youth at Sir Ector's castle in the Forest Sauvage, where Merlyn the magician introduced him to the political ideologies found in the animal kingdom by temporarily transforming him into various beasts, Arthur was placed on the throne by destiny, compelled by his sense of justice and harmony to create the "civilized world" and the famous Round Table, to stimulate the Quest for the Holy Grail in an effort to keep man from killing man.

But a darker fate also dictated his ignorant siring of an illegitimate son by his own half sister and forced his wife Guenever and his best knight Lancelot into each other's arms, thus causing rivalry, deceit, and jealousy among the knights.

These last proved to be the old king's downfall. Forgotten were his achievements for the Might of Right and for peace on earth. Forgotten too was his own anguish at having tried his best and failed. The Quest had led nowhere, the Round Table was dispersed. Now Guenever was besieged by Mordred and his Thrashers in the Tower of London and Lancelot was exiled in France, both victims of Mordred's obsession to gain Arthur's throne.

So now Arthur is alone, fulfilling his royal duties by absentmindedly going through the day's paperwork, feeling his losses and his pain. He looks up at a movement at his tent door.

The Book of Merlyn

Incipit Liber Quintus

He thought a little and said:
* "I have found the Zoological Gardens*
of service to many of my patients.
I should prescribe for Mr. Pontifex
a course of the larger mammals.
Don't let him think he is taking them
medicinally...."

1

IT WAS NOT the Bishop of Rochester.

The king turned his head away from the newcomer, incurious as to his identity. The tears, running down his loose cheeks with their slow plods, made him feel ashamed to be seen: yet he was too vanquished to check them. He turned stubbornly from the light, unable to do more. He had reached the stage at which it was not worthwhile to hide an old man's misery.

Merlyn sat down beside him and took the worn hand, which made the tears flow faster. The magician patted the hand, holding it quietly with a thumb on its blue veins, waiting for life to revive.

"Merlyn?" asked the king.

He did not seem to be surprised.

"Are you a dream?" he asked. "Last night I dreamed that Gawaine came to me, with a troupe of fair ladies. He said they were allowed to come with him, because he had rescued them in his lifetime, and they had come to warn us that we should all be killed tomorrow. Then I had another dream, that I was sitting on a throne strapped to the top of a wheel, and the wheel turned over, and I was thrown into a pit of snakes."

"The wheel is come full circle: I am here."

"Are you a bad dream?" he asked. "If you are, do not torment me."

Merlyn still held the hand. He stroked along the veins, trying to make them sink into the flesh. He soothed the flaky skin and poured life into it with mysterious concentration, encouraging it to resilience. He tried to make the body flexible under his finger-tips, helping the blood to course, putting a bloom and smoothness on the swollen joints, but not speaking.

"You are a good dream," said the king. "I hope you will go on dreaming."

"I am not a dream at all. I am the man whom you remembered."

"Oh, Merlyn, it has been so miserable since you left! Everything which you helped to do was wrong. All your teaching was deception. Nothing was worth doing. You and I will be forgotten, like people who never were."

"Forgotten?" asked the magician. He smiled in the candle light, looking round the tent as if to assure himself of its furs and twinkling mail and the tapestries and vellums.

"There was a king," he said, "whom Nennius wrote about, and Geoffrey of Monmouth. The Archdeacon of Oxford was said to have had a hand in him, and even that delightful ass, Gerald

the Welshman. Brut, Layamon and the rest of
them: what a lot of lies they all managed to tell!
Some said that he was a Briton painted blue, some
that he was in chain mail to suit the ideas of the
Norman romancers. Certain lumbering Germans
dressed him up to vie with their tedious Siegfrieds.
Others put him into plate, like your friend
Thomas of Hutton Coniers, and others again,
notably a romantic Elizabethan called Hughes,
recognised his extraordinary problem of love.
Then there was a blind poet who tried to justify
God's ways to man, and he weighed Arthur
against Adam, wondering which was more
important of the two. At the same time came
masters of music like Purcell, and later still such
titans as the Romantics, endlessly dreaming about
our king. There came men who dressed him in
armour like ivy-leaves, and who made all his
friends to stand about among ruins with brambles
twining round them, or else to swoon backward
with a mellow blur kissing them on the lips. Also
there was Victoria's lord. Even the most unlikely
people meddled with him, people like Aubrey
Beardsley, who illustrated his history. After a bit
there was poor old White, who thought that we
represented the ideas of chivalry. He said that our
importance lay in our decency, in our resistance
against the bloody mind of man. What an
anachronist he was, dear fellow! Fancy starting
after William the Conqueror, and ending in the
Wars of the Roses... Then there were people who
turned out the *Morte d'Arthur* in mystic waves
like the wireless, and others in an undiscovered
hemisphere who still pretended that Arthur and

Merlyn were the natural fathers of themselves in
pictures which would move. The Matter of
Britain! Certainly we were forgotten, Arthur, if a
thousand years and half a thousand, and yet a
thousand years again, are to be the measure of
forgetfulness."

"Who is this Wight?"

"A fellow," replied the magician absently. "Just
listen, will you, while I recite a piece from
Kipling?" And the old gentleman proceeded to
intone with passion the famous paragraph out of
Pook's Hill: "'I've seen Sir Huon and a troop of
his people setting off from Tintagel Castle for Hy-
Brasil in the teeth of a sou'-westerly gale, with the
spray flying all over the castle, and the Horses of
the Hill wild with fright. Out they'd go in a lull,
screaming like gulls, and back they'd be driven
five good miles inland before they could come
head to wind again.... It was Magic—Magic as
black as Merlin could make it, and the whole sea
was green fire and white foam with singing
mermaids in it. And the Horses of the Hill picked
their way from one wave to another by the
lightning flashes! *That* was how it was in the old
days!'

"There is description for you," he added, when
he had finished the piece. "There is prose. No
wonder that Dan cried 'Splendid!' at the end of it.
And all was written about ourselves or about our
friends."

"But Master, I do not understand."

The magician stood up, looking at his ancient
pupil in perplexity. He twisted his beard into

several rat tails, put the corners in his mouth,
twirled his moustachios, and cracked his finger
joints. He was frightened of what he had done to
the king, feeling as if he were trying to revive a
drowned man with artificial respiration, who was
nearly too far gone. But he was not ashamed.
When you are a scientist you must press on
without remorse, following the only thing of any
importance, Truth.

Later he asked quietly, as if he were calling
somebody who was asleep: "Wart?"

There was no reply.

"King?"

The bitter answer was: *"Le roy s'advisera."*

It was worse than he had feared. He sat down,
took the limp hand, and began to wheedle.

"One more try," he asked. "We are not quite
done."

"What is the use of trying?"

"It is a thing which people do."

"People are dupes, then."

The old fellow replied frankly: "People are
dupes, and wicked too. That is what makes it
interesting to get them better."

His victim opened his eyes, but closed them
wearily.

"The thing which you were thinking about
before I came, king, was true. I mean about
Homo ferox. But hawks are *ferae naturae* also:
that is their interest."

The eyes remained closed.

"The thing which you were thinking
about...about people being machines: that was

not true. Or, if it is true, it does not signify. For if we are all machines ourselves, then there are none to bother about."

"I see."

Curiously enough, he did see. Also his eyes came open and remained open.

"Do you remember the angel in the Bible, who was ready to spare whole cities provided that one just man could be found? Was it one? That applies to *Homo ferox,* Arthur, even now."

The eyes began to watch their vision closely.

"You have been taking my advice too literally, king. To disbelieve in original sin, does not mean that you must believe in original virtue. It only means that you must not believe that people are utterly wicked. Wicked they may be, and even very wicked, but not utterly. Otherwise, I agree, it would be no use trying."

Arthur said, with one of his sweet smiles: "This is a good dream. I hope it will be long."

His teacher took out his spectacles, polished them, put them on his nose, and examined the old man carefully. There was a hint of satisfaction behind the lenses.

"Unless," he said, "you had lived this, you would not have known it. One has to live one's knowledge. How are you?"

"Fairly well. How are you?"

"Very well."

They shook hands, as if they had just met.

"Will you be staying?"

"Actually," replied the necromancer, now blowing his nose furiously in order to hide his glee, or perhaps to hide his contrition, "I shall

hardly be here at all. I have been sent with an
invitation."

He folded his handkerchief and replaced it in
his cap.

"Any mice?" asked the king with a first faint
twinkle. The skin of his face twitched as it were,
or tautened itself for the fraction of a second, so
that you could see underneath it, in the bone
perhaps, the freckled, snub-nosed countenance of
a little boy who had once been charmed by
Archimedes.

Merlyn took the skull-cap off indulgently.

"One," he said. "I think it was a mouse: but it
has become partly shrivelled. And here, I see, is
the frog I picked up in the summer. It had been
run over, poor creature, during the drought. A
perfect silhouette."

He examined it complacently before putting it
back, then crossed his legs and examined his
companion in the same way, nursing his knee.

"The invitation," he said. "We were hoping you
would pay us a visit. Your battle can look after
itself until tomorrow, we suppose?"

"Nothing matters in a dream."

This seemed to anger him, for he exclaimed
with some vexation: "I wish you would stop about
dreams! You must consider other people."

"Never mind."

"The invitation, then. It was to visit my cave,
where young Nimue put me. Do you remember
her? There are some friends in it, waiting to meet
you."

"It would be beautiful."

"Your battle is arranged, I believe, and you

would hardly sleep in any case. It might cheer your heart to come."

"Nothing is arranged," said the king. "But dreams arrange themselves."

At this the aged gentleman leaped from his seat, clutching his forehead as if he had been shot in it, and raised his wand of libnum vitae to the skies.

"Merciful powers! Dreams again!"

He took off his conical hat with a stately gesture, looked piercingly upon the bearded figure opposite which looked as old as he did, and banged himself on the head with his wand as a mark of exclamation. Then he sat down, half stunned, having misjudged the emphasis.

The old king watched him with a warming mind. Now that he was dreaming of his long-lost friend so vividly, he began to see why Merlyn had always clowned on purpose. It had been a means of helping people to learn in a happy way. He began to feel the greatest affection, which was even mixed with awe, for his tutor's ancient courage: which could go on believing and trying with undaunted crankiness, in spite of ages of experience. He began to be lightened at the thought that benevolence and valour could persist. In the lightening of his heart he smiled, closed his eyes, and dropped asleep in earnest.

2

WHEN HE OPENED THEM, it was still dark. Merlyn was there, moodily scratching the greyhound's ears and muttering. He had saved his pupil from misery before, by being nasty to him when he was a young boy called the Wart, but he knew that the poor old chap before him now had suffered too much misery for the trick to work again. The next best thing was to distract the king's attention, he must have decided, for he set to work as soon as the eyes were open, in a way which all magicians understand. They are accustomed to palm things off on people, under a mirage of patter.

"Now," he said. "Dreams. We must get this over for good and all. Apart from the maddening indignity of being called a dream—personally, because it muddles you—it confuses other people. How about the learned readers? And it is degrading to ourselves. When I was a third-rate schoolmaster in the twentieth century—or was it

in the nineteenth—every single boy I ever met
wrote essays for me which ended: Then he woke
up. You could say that the Dream was the only
literary convention of their most degraded
classrooms. Are we to be this? We are the Matter
of Britain, remember. And what of
oneirocriticism, I ask? What are the psychologists
to make of it? Stuff as dreams are made of is stuff
and nonsense in my opinion."

"Yes," said the king meekly.

"Do I look like a dream?"

"Yes."

Merlyn seemed to gasp with vexation, then put
the whole beard into his mouth at one mouthful.
After this he blew his nose and went away to
stand in a corner, with his face to the canvas,
where he began to soliloquise indignantly.

"Of all the persecutions and floutings," he
stated. "How can a necromancer prove he is not a
vision, when suspected of the baseness? A ghost
may prove he is alive by being pinched: but not so
with a by-our-lady dream. For, argal, you can
dream of pinches. Yet hist! There is the noted
remedy, in which the dreamer pinches his own leg.

"Arthur," he directed, turning round like a top,
"be pleased to pinch yourself."

"Yes."

"Now, does this prove you are awake?"

"I doubt it."

The vision examined him sadly.

"I was afraid it would not," it agreed; and it
returned to its corner, where it began to recite
some complicated passages from Burton, Jung,
Hippocrates and Sir Thomas Browne.

After five minutes, it struck its fist into the palm of the other hand and marched back to the candle light, inspired by the bed of Cleopatra.

"Listen," Merlyn announced. "Have you ever dreamed of a smell?"

"Dreamed of a smell?"

"Do not repeat."

"I can hardly..."

"Come, come. You have dreamed of a sight, have you not? And of a feeling: everybody has dreamed of a feeling. You may even have dreamed of a taste. I recollect that once when I had forgotten to eat anything for a fortnight, I dreamed of a chocolate pudding: which I distinctly tasted, but it was snatched away. The question is, have you ever dreamed of a smell?"

"I do not think I have: not to smell it."

"Make sure. Do not stare like an idiot, my dear man, but attend to the matter in hand. Have you ever dreamed with your nose?"

"Never. I cannot remember dreaming of a smell."

"You are positive?"

"Positive."

"Then smell that!" cried the necromancer, snatching off his skull-cap and presenting it under Arthur's nose, with its cargo of mice, frogs and a few shrimps for salmon-fishing which he had overlooked.

"Phew!"

"Am I a dream now?"

"It does not smell like one."

"Well, then..."

"Merlyn," said the king. "It makes no

difference whether you are a dream or not, so long as you are here. Sit down and be patient for a little, if you can. Tell me the reason of your visit. Talk. Say you have come to save us from this war."

The old fellow had achieved his object of artificial respiration as well as he could; so now he sat down comfortably, and took the matter in hand.

"No," he said. "Nobody can be saved from anything, unless they save themselves. It is hopeless doing things for people—it is often very dangerous indeed to do things at all—and the only thing worth doing for the race is to increase its stock of ideas. Then, if you make available a larger stock, the people are at liberty to help themselves from out of it. By this process the means of improvement is offered, to be accepted or rejected freely, and there is a faint hope of progress in the course of the millennia. Such is the business of the philosopher, to open new ideas. It is not his business to impose them on people."

"You did not tell me this before."

"Why not?"

"You have egged me into doing things during all my life . . . The Chivalry and the Round Table which you made me invent, what were these but efforts to save people, and to get things done?"

"They were ideas," said the philosopher firmly, "rudimentary ideas. All thought, in its early stages, begins as action. The actions which you have been wading through have been ideas, clumsy ones of course, but they had to be established as a foundation before we could begin to think in earnest. You have been teaching man to think in action. Now it is time to think in our heads."

"So my Table was not a failure—Master?"

"Certainly not. It was an experiment. Experiments lead to new ones, and this is why I have come to take you to our burrow."

"I am ready," he said, amazed to find that he was feeling happy.

"The Committee discovered that there had been some gaps in your education, two of them, and it was determined that these ought to be put right before concluding the active stage of the Idea."

"What is this committee? It sounds as if they had been making a report."

"And so we did. You will meet them presently in the cave. But now, excuse my mentioning it, there is a matter to arrange before we go."

Here Merlyn examined his toes with a doubtful eye, hesitating to continue.

"Men's brains," he explained in the end, "seem to get petrified as they grow older. The surface becomes perished, like worn leather, and will no longer take impressions. You may have noticed it?"

"I feel a stiffness in my head."

"Now children have resilient, plastic brains," continued the magician with relish, as if he were talking about caviare sandwiches. "They can take impressions before you could say Jack Robinson. To learn a language when you are young, for instance, might literally be called child's play: but after middle age one finds it is the devil."

"I have heard people say so."

"What the committee suggested was, that if you are to learn these things we speak of, you ought—ahem—you ought to be a boy. They have furnished me with a patent medicine to do it. You understand: you would become the Wart once more."

"Not if I had to live my life again," replied the other old fellow evenly.

They faced each other like image and object in a mirror, the outside corners of their eyes drawn down with the hooded lids of age.

"It would be only for the evening."

"The Elixir of Life?"

"Exactly. Think of the people who have tried to find it."

"If I were to find such a thing, I would throw it away."

"I hope you are not being stupid about children," asked Merlyn, looking vaguely about him. "We have high authority for being born again, like little ones. Grown-ups have developed an unpleasant habit lately, I notice, of comforting themselves for their degradation by pretending that children are childish. I trust we are free from this?"

"Everybody knows that children are more intelligent than their parents."

"You and I know it, but the people who are going to read this book do not."

"Our readers of that time," continued the necromancer in a grim voice, "have exactly three ideas in their magnificent noodles. The first is that the human species is superior to others. The second, that the twentieth century is superior to other centuries. And the third, that human adults of the twentieth century are superior to their young. The whole illusion may be labelled Progress, and anybody who questions it is called puerile, reactionary, or an escapist. The March of Mind, God help them."

He considered these facts for some time, then added: "And a fourth piece of scientific clap-trap which they are to have, rejoices in the name of anthropomorphism. Even their children are supposed to be so superior to the animals that you must never mention the two creatures in the same breath. If you begin considering men as animals, they put it the other way round and say that you are considering animals as men, a sin which they hold to be worse than bigamy. Imagine a scientist being merely an animal, they say! Tut-tut, and Tilly-fol-de-rido!"

"Who are these readers?"

"The readers of the book."

"What book?"

"The book we are in."

"Are we in a book?"

"We had better attend to the job," said Merlyn hastily.

He took hold of his wand, rolled up his sleeves, and fixed a tight eye on the patient. "Do you agree?" he asked.

But the old king stopped him.

"No," he said, with a sort of firm apology. "I have earned my body and mind with many years of labour. It would be undignified to change them. I am not too proud to be a child, Merlyn,

but too old. If it were my body which were to be
made young, it would be unsuitable to keep an
old mind in it. While, if you were to change them
both, the labour of living all those years would
turn to vanity. There is nothing else for it, Master.
We must keep the state of life to which it has
pleased God to call us."

The magician lowered the wand.

"But your brain," he complained. "It is like a
fossilised sponge. And would you not have liked
to be young, to frisk about and feel your knees
again? Young people are happy, are they not? We
had meant it for a pleasure."

"It would indeed have been a pleasure, and
thank you for thinking of it. But life is not
invented for happiness, I do believe. It is made for
something else."

Merlyn chewed the end of his stick while he
considered.

"You are right," he said in the end. "I was
against the proposal from the start. But something
will have to be done to souple your intellects, for
all that, or you will never catch the new idea. I
suppose there would be no objection to a cerebral
massage, if I could manage it? I should have to get
my galvanic batteries, my extra-reds and under-
violets: my french chalk and my pinches of this
and that: a touch of adrenalin and a sniff of
garlic. You know the kind of thing?"

"No, if you think it is right."

He extended his hand into the ether, with a
well-remembered gesture, and the apparatus
began to materialise obediently: muddled up as
usual.

3

THE TREATMENT WAS UNPLEASANT. It was like having one's hair brushed vigorously the wrong way, or like having a sprained ankle flexed by that dreadful kind of masseuse who urges people to relax. The king gripped the arms of his chair, closed his eyes, clenched his teeth and sweated. When he opened them for the second time that evening, it was on a different world.

"Good heavens!" he exclaimed, jumping to his feet. In leaving the chair he did not take his weight upon his wrists, like an old man, but upon the palms and phalanges. "Look at the dog's hollow eyes! The candles are reflected from the back, not from the front, as if it were from the bottom of a cup. Why have I never noticed this before? And look here: there is a hole in Bathsheba's bath, which needs darning. What is this entry in the book? *Susp.?** Who has betrayed

---

*Abbreviation for *suspendatur,* "let him be hanged."

us into hanging people? Nobody deserves to be
hanged. Merlyn, why is there no reflection from
your eyes, when I put the candles between us?
Why have I never thought about it? The light
comes red from a fox, green from a cat, yellow
from a horse, saffron from a dog... And look at
that falcon's beak: it has a tooth in it like a saw!
Goshawks and sparrow-hawks do not have a
tooth. It must be a peculiarity of *falco*. What an
extraordinary thing a tent is! Half of it is trying to
push it up, and the other half is trying to pull it
down. *Ex nihilo res fit.* † And look at those chess-
men! Check-mate indeed! Nay, we will try the
ploy again..."

Imagine a rusty bolt on the garden door, which
has been set wrong, or the door has sagged on its
hinges since it was put on, and for years that bolt
has never been shot efficiently: except by
hammering it, or by lifting the door a little, and
wriggling it home with effort. Imagine then that
the old bolt is unscrewed, rubbed with emery
paper, bathed in paraffin, polished with fine sand,
generously oiled, and reset by a skilled workman
with such nicety that it bolts and unbolts with the
pressure of a finger—with the pressure of a
feather—almost so that you could blow it open or
shut. Can you imagine the feelings of the bolt?
They are the feelings of glory which convalescent
people have, after a fever. It would look forward

---

†"Something comes of nothing." This is a parody or
adaptation of *ex nihilo nihil fit,* that is, "nothing comes of
nothing," familiar (though not in that exact form) from both
Lucretius and Persius.

to being bolted, yearning for the rapture of its sweet, successful motion.

For happiness is only a bye-product of function, as light is a bye-product of the electric current running through the wires. If the current cannot run efficiently, the light does not come. That is why nobody finds happiness, who seeks it on its own account. But man must seek to be like the working bolt; like the unimpeded run of electricity; like the convalescent whose eyes, long thwarted in their sockets by headache and fever, so that it was a grievous pain to move them, now flash from side to side with the ease of clean fishes in clear water. The eyes are working, the current is working, the bolt is working. So the light shines. That is happiness: working well.

"Hold hard," said Merlyn. "After all, we have no train to catch."

"No train?"

"I beg your pardon. It is a quotation which a friend of mine used to apply to human progress. However, as you look as if you were feeling better, shall we start for the cave at once?"

"Immediately."

They made no further ado but lifted the tent-flap and were gone, leaving the sleeping greyhound to watch the hooded hawk in solitude. Hearing the tent-flap lift, the blinded bird screamed out in raucous accents for attention.

It was a bracing walk for both of them. The wild wind and the speed of their passage tugged their beards to left or right over their shoulders, accordingly as they did not face exactly into the eye of it, which gave a tight feeling at the hair-roots, as if they were in curl papers. They sped over Salisbury plain, past the thought-provoking monument of Stonehenge, where Merlyn, in passing, cried a salutation to the old gods whom Arthur could not see: to Crom, Bell and others. They whirled over Wiltshire, strode beyond Dorset and sped through Devon, as fast as a wire cutting cheese. The plains, downs, forests, moors and hillocks fell behind them. The glinting rivers swung past like the spokes of a turning wheel. In Cornwall they halted, by the side of an ancient tumulus like an enormous mole-hill, with a dark opening in its side.

"We go in."

"I have been to this place before," said the king, standing still in a kind of catalepsy.

"Yes."

"When?"

"When yourself?"

He groped, searched in his mind, feeling that the revelation was in his heart. But "No," he said, "I cannot remember."

"Come and see."

They went down the labyrinthine passages, past the turnings which led to the bedchambers, to the middens, to the storerooms and to the place where you went if you wanted to wash your hands. At last the king stopped, with his fingers on the door latch at the end of a passage, and announced: "I know where I am."

Merlyn watched.

"It is the badger's sett, where I went when I was a child."

"Yes."

"Merlyn, you villain! I have been mourning you for half a lifetime, because I thought you were shut up like a toad in a hole, and all the time you have been sitting in the Combination Room, arguing with badger!"

"Open the door, and look."

He opened it. There was the well-remembered room. There were the portraits of long-dead badgers, famous for scholarship or godliness: there were the glow-worms and the mahogany fans and the tilting board for circulating the decanters. There were the moth-eaten gowns and the chairs of stamped leather. But, best of all, there were his earliest friends—the preposterous committee.

They were rising shyly to their feet to greet him. They were confused in their humble feelings, partly because they had been looking forward to the surprise so much, and partly because they had never met real kings before—so that they were afraid he might be different. Still, they were determined that they ought to do the thing in style. They had arranged that the proper thing would be to stand up, and perhaps to bow or smile a bit. There had been solemn consultations among them about whether he ought to be addressed as "Your Majesty" or as "Sir," about whether his hand ought to be kissed, about whether he would be much changed, and even, poor souls, about whether he would remember them at all.

They were there in a circle round the fire: badger hoisting himself bashfully to his feet while

a perfect avalanche of manuscript shot out of his
lap into the fender: T. natrix uncoiling himself
and flickering an ebon tongue, with which he
proposed to kiss the royal hand if necessary:
Archimedes bobbing up and down with pleasure
and anticipation, half spreading his wings and
causing them to flutter, like a small bird asking to
be fed: Balin looking crushed for the first time in
his life, because he was afraid he might have been
forgotten: Cavall, so agonised by the glory of his
feelings that he had to go away into a corner and
be sick: goat, who had given the emperor's salute
in a flash of foresight long before: hedgehog
standing loyal and erect at the bottom of the
circle, where he had been made to sit apart from
the others on account of his fleas, but full of
patriotism and anxiety to be noticed if possible.
Even the enormous stuffed pike, which was a
novelty over the mantelpiece beneath the
Founder, seemed to regard him with a
supplicating eye.

"Oh, people!" exclaimed the king.

Then they all flushed a great deal, and shuffled
their feet, and said that he must please to excuse
their humble home, or Welcome to Your Majesty,
or We did mean to put up a banner only it had
got lost, or Are your regal feet wet? or Here
comes the squire, or Oh, it is so lovely to see you
after all these years! Hedgehog saluted stiffly,
saying "Rule Britannia!"

The next moment a rejuvenated Arthur was
shaking hands with all, kissing them and
thumping them on the back, until the tears stood
in every eye.

"We did not know..." sniffed the badger.

"We were afraid you might have forgot..."

"Do we say Your Majesty, or do we say Sir?"

He sensibly answered the question on its merits.

"It is Your Majesty for an emperor, but for an ordinary king it is Sir."

So from that moment they thought of him as the Wart, without considering the matter further.

When the excitement had died down, Merlyn closed the door and took control of the situation.

"Now," he said. "We have a great deal of business to transact, and very little time to do it in. Here you are, king: here is a chair for you at the head of the circle, because you are our leader, who does the hard work and suffers the pains. And you, urchin, it is your turn to be Ganymede, so you had better fetch the madeira wine and be quick about it. Hand round a big cup for everybody, and then we will start the meeting."

Hedgehog brought the first cup to Arthur, and served him with importance on a bended knee, keeping one grubby thumb in the glass. Then, while he moved off round the circle, the some-time Wart had leisure to look about him.

The Combination Room had changed since his last visit, a change which hinted strongly at his tutor's personality. For there, on all the spare chairs and on the floor and on the tables, lying open to mark significant passages, were thousands of books of all descriptions, each one forgotten since it had been laid down for future reference, and all covered with a fine layer of dust. There was Thierry and Pinnow and Gibbon and

Sigismondi and Duruy and Prescott and Parkman
and Juserand and d'Alton and Tacitus and Smith
and Trevelyan and Herodotus and Dean Millman
and MacAllister and Geoffrey of Monmouth and
Wells and Clausewitz and Giraldus Cambrensis—
including the lost volumes on England and
Scotland—and Tolstoy's *War and Peace* and the
Comic History of England and the *Saxon
Chronicle* and the *Four Masters.* There were de
Beer's *Vertebrate Zoology,* Elliott-Smith's *Essays
on the Evolution of Man,* Eltringham's *Senses of
Insects,* Browne's *Vulgar Errors,* Aldrovandus,
Matthew Paris, a Bestiary by Physiologus, Frazer
in the complete edition, and even *Zeus* by A. B.
Cook. There were encyclopedias, charts of the
human and other bodies, reference books like
Witherby, about every sort of bird and animal,
dictionaries, logarithm tables, and the whole series
of the *D.N.B.* On one wall there was a digest
made out in Merlyn's longhand, which shewed, in
parallel columns, a concordance of the histories of
the human races for the last ten thousand years.
The Assyrians, Sumerians, Mongols, Aztecs etc.
each had a separate ink, and the year A.D. or B.C.
was written on a vertical line at the left of the
columns, so that it was like a graph. Then, on
another wall, which was even more interesting,
there was a real graph which shewed the rise and
fall of various animal races for the last thousand
million years. When a race became extinct, its line
met the horizontal asymptote and vanished. One
of the latest to do this was the Irish elk. A map,
done for fun, shewed the position of the local
birds' nests in the previous spring. In a corner of

the room remote from the fire, there was a worktable with a microscope on it, under whose lens there was laid out an exquisite piece of micro-dissection, the nervous system of an ant. On the same table there were the skulls of men, apes, fish and wild geese, also dissected, in order to shew the relation between neopallium and corpus striatum. Another corner was fitted up with a sort of laboratory, in which, in indescribable confusion, there stood retorts, test tubes, centrifuges, germ-cultures, beakers and bottles labelled Pituitary, Adrenalin, Furniture Polish, Venticatchellum's Curry Powder, or De Kuyper's Gin. The latter had a pencilled inscription on the label, which said: The Level on this Bottle is MARKED. Finally there were meat-safes containing live specimens of mantes, locusts and other insects, while the remainder of the floor carried a débris of the magician's passing crazes. There were croquet mallets, knitting needles, pastels surfins, lino-cutting tools, kites, boomerangs, glue, boxes of cigars, home-made wood-wind instruments, cookery books, a bull-roarer, a telescope, a tin of grafting wax and a hamper marked Fortnum and Mason's on the bottom.

The old king heaved a sigh of contentment, and forgot about the actual world.

"Now, badger," said Merlyn, who was bristling with importance and officiousness, "hand me the minutes of the last meeting."

"We did not take any. There was no ink."

"Never mind. Give me the notes on the Great Victorian Hubris."

"They were used to light the fire."

"Confound it. Then pass the *Prophecies*."

"Here they are," said the badger proudly, and he stooped down to scrape together the flood of papers which had shot into the fender when he first stood up. "I had them ready," he explained, "on purpose."

They had caught light, however, and, when he had blown them out and delivered them to the magician, it was found that all the pages had been burned in half.

"Really, this is too vexatious! What have you done with the Thesis on Man, and the Dissertation Concerning Might?"

"I had them under my hand a moment ago."

And the poor badger, who was supposed to be the secretary of the committee, but he was not a good one, began rummaging about short-sightedly among the boomerangs, looking very much ashamed and worried.

Archimedes said, "It might be easier to do it without papers, Master, just by talking."

Merlyn glared at him.

"We have only to explain," suggested T. natrix.

Merlyn glared at him also.

"It is what we shall have to do in the end," said Balin, "in any case."

Merlyn gave up glaring and went into the sulks.

Cavall, who had come secretly, sneaked into the king's lap with an imploring look, and was not prevented. Goat stared into the fire with his jewel eyes. Badger sat down again with a guilty expression, and hedgehog, sitting primly in his corner away from the others with his hands folded in his lap, gave an unexpected lead.

"Tell 'un," he said.

Everybody looked at him in surprise, but he was not to be put down. He knew why people moved away when he sat next to them, but a mun had rights for all that.

"Tell 'un," he repeated.

The king said, "I would like it very much if you did tell me. At present I do not understand anything, except that I have been brought here to fill some gaps in this extraordinary education. Could you explain from the beginning?"

"The trouble is," said Archimedes, "that it is difficult to decide which is the beginning."

"Tell me about the committee, then. Why are you a committee, and what on?"

"You could say we are the Committee on Might in Man. We have been trying to understand your puzzle."

"It is a Royal Commission," explained the badger proudly. "It was felt that a mixture of animals would be able to advise upon the different departments..."

Here Merlyn could contain himself no longer. Even for the sake of his sulks, it was impossible to hold off when it came to talking.

"Allow me," he said. "I know exactly where to begin, and now I shall do it. Everybody to listen.

"My dear Wart," he continued, after the hedgehog had said Hear-hear and, as an afterthought, Order-order, "I must ask you at the outset to cast your mind back to the beginning of my tutorship. Can you remember?"

"It was with animals."

"Exactly. And has it occurred to you that this was not for fun?"

"Well, it was fun...."

"But why, we are asking you, with animals?"

"Suppose you were to tell me."

The magician crossed his knees, folded his arms and frowned with importance.

"There are two hundred and fifty thousand separate species of animal in this world," he said, "not counting the living vegetables, and of these no less than two thousand eight hundred and fifty are mammals like man. They all of them have some form of politics or another—it was the one mistake my old friend Aristotle made, when he defined his man as a Political Animal—yet man himself, this miserable nonentity among two hundred and forty-nine thousand nine hundred and ninety-nine others, goes drivelling along his tragic political groove, without ever lifting his eyes to the quarter million examples which surround him. What makes it still more extraordinary is that man is a parvenu among the rest, nearly all of which had already solved his problems in one way or another, many thousand years before he was created."

There was a murmur of admiration from the committee, and the grass-snake added gently: "It was why he tried to give you an idea of nature, king, because it was hoped that when you were struggling with the puzzle, you would look about you."

"The politics of all animals," said the badger, "deal with the control of Might."

"But I do not see..." he began, only to be anticipated.

"Of course you do not see," said Merlyn. "You were going to say that animals have no politics. Take my advice, and think it over."

"Have they?"

"Of course they have, and very efficient ones they are. Some of them are communists or fascists, like many of the ants: some are anarchists, like the geese. There are socialists like some of the bees, and, indeed, among the three thousand families of the ant itself, there are other shades of ideology besides fascism. Not all are slave-makers or warfarers. There are bank-balance-holders like the squirrel, or the bear who hibernates on his fat. Any nest or burrow or feeding ground is a form of individual property, and how do you think the crows, rabbits, minnows, and all the other gregarious creatures contrive to live together, if they have not faced the questions of Democracy and of Force?"

It was evidently a well-worn topic, for the badger interrupted before the king could reply.

"You have never given us," he said, "and you never will give us, an example of capitalism in the natural world."

Merlyn looked unhappy.

"And," he added, "if you cannot give an example, it only shews that capitalism is unnatural."

The badger, it may be mentioned, was inclined to be Russian in his outlook. He and the other animals had argued with the magician so much during the past few centuries that they had all

come to express themselves in highly magic terms,
talking of bolshevists and nazis with as much ease
as if they had been little more than the Lollards
and Thrashers of contemporary history.

Merlyn, who was a staunch conservative—
which was rather progressive of him, when you
reflect that he was living backwards—defended
himself feebly.

"Parasitism," he said, "is an ancient and

respectable compartment in nature, from the cuckoo to the flea."

"We are not talking about parasitism. We are talking about capitalism, which has been exactly defined. Can you give me a single example, other than man, of a species whose individuals will exploit the labour value of individuals of the same species? Even fleas do not exploit fleas."

Merlyn said: "There are certain apes which, when kept in captivity, have to be closely watched by their keepers. Otherwise the dominant individuals will deprive their comrades of food, even compelling them to regurgitate it, and the comrades will starve."

"It seems a shaky example."

Merlyn folded his hands and looked more unhappy than ever. At last he screwed his courage to the sticking point, took a deep breath, and faced the truth.

"It is a shaky example," he said. "I find it impossible to mention an example of true capitalism in nature."

He had no sooner said it than his hands unfolded themselves like lightning, and the fist of one flashed into the palm of the other.

"I have it!" he cried. "I knew I was right about capitalism. We are looking at it the wrong way round."

"We generally are."

"The main specialisation of a species is nearly always unnatural to other species. Just because there are no examples of capital in nature, it does not mean that capital is unnatural for man, in the sense of its being wrong. You might as well say that it is wrong for a giraffe to eat the tops of trees, because there are no other antelopes with necks as long as his, or that it was wrong for the first amphibian to crawl out of the water, because there were no other examples of amphibians at the time. Capitalism is man's speciality, just as his cerebrum is. There are no other examples in nature of a creature with a cerebrum like that of man. This does not mean that it is unnatural for man to have a cerebrum. On the contrary, it means that he must go ahead with it. And the same with his capitalism. It is, like his brain, a speciality, a jewel in the crown! Now I come to think of it, capitalism may be actually consequent upon the possession of a developed cerebrum. Otherwise, who should our only other example of capitalism—those apes I mentioned—occur among the anthropoids whose brains are akin to man's? Yes, yes, I knew I was right to be a minor capitalist all the time. I knew there was a sensible reason why the Russians of my youth should have modified their ideas. The fact that it is unique does not mean that it is wrong: on the contrary, it means that it is right. Right for man, of course, not for the other animals. It means..."

"Do you realise," asked Archimedes, "that the audience has not understood a single word you are saying, for several minutes?"

Merlyn stopped abruptly and looked at his pupil, who had been following the conversation with his eyes more than anything else, looking from one face to the other.

"I am sorry."

The king spoke absently, almost as if he were talking to himself.

"Have I been stupid?" he asked slowly, "stupid not to notice animals?"

"Stupid!" cried the magician, triumphant once again, for he was in high delight over his discovery about capital. "There at last is a crumb of truth on a pair of human lips! *Nunc dimittis!*"*

And he immediately leaped upon his hobby-horse, to gallop off in all directions.

"The cheek of the human race," he exclaimed, "is something to knock you footless. Begin with the unthinkable universe; narrow down to the minute sun inside it; pass to the satellite of the sun which we are pleased to call the Earth; glance at the myriad algae, or whatever the things are called, of the sea, and at the uncountable microbes, going backwards to a minus infinity, which populate ourselves. Drop an eye on those quarter million other species which I have mentioned, and upon the unmentionable expanses of time through which they have lived. Then look at man, an upstart whose eyes, speaking from the point of view of nature, are scarcely open further than the puppy's. There he is, the—the gollywog—" He was becoming so excited that he had no time to think of suitable epithets. "There he is, dubbing himself *Homo sapiens,* forsooth, proclaiming himself the lord of creation, like that

_____

*Literally, "now you send away" or "now you let depart," from the Canticle of Simeon, Luke 2:29. This has come to be used in a general sense, signifying "I've seen it all now; I can die happy."

ass Napoleon putting on his own crown! There he
is, condescending to the other animals: even
condescending, God bless my soul and body, to
his ancestors! It is the Great Victorian Hubris, the
amazing, ineffable presumption of the nineteenth
century. Look at those historical novels by Scott,
in which the human beings themselves, because
they lived a couple of hundred years ago, are
made to talk like imitation warming pans! Man,
proud man, stands there in the twentieth century,
complacently believing that the race has
'advanced' in the course of a thousand miserable
years, and busy blowing his brothers to bits.
When will they learn that it takes a million years
for a bird to modify a single one of its primary
feathers? There he stands, the crashing lubber,
pretending that everything is different because
he has made an internal combustion engine. There
he stands, ever since Darwin, because he has
heard that there is such a thing as evolution. Quite
regardless of the fact that evolution happens in
million-year cycles, he thinks he has evolved since
the Middle Ages. Perhaps the combustion engine
has evolved, but not he. Look at him sniggering at
his own progenitors, let alone the other types of
mammal, in that insufferable *Connecticut Yankee
in King Arthur's Court*. The sheer, shattering
sauce of it! And making God in his own image!
Believe me, the so-called primitive races who
worshipped animals as gods were not so daft as
people choose to pretend. At least they were
humble. Why should not God have come to the
earth as an earth-worm? There are a great many
more worms than men, and they do a great deal

more good. And what is it all about, anyway? Where is this marvellous superiority which makes the twentieth century superior to the Middle Ages, and the Middle Ages superior to primitive races and to the beasts of the field? Is man so particularly good at controlling his Might and his Ferocity and his Property? What does he do? He massacres the members of his own species like a cannibal! Do you know that it has been calculated that, during the years between 1100 and 1900, the English were at war for four hundred and nineteen years and the French for three hundred and seventy-three? Do you know that Lapouge has reckoned that nineteen million men are killed in Europe in every century, so that the amount of blood spilled would feed a fountain of blood running seven hundred litres an hour since the beginning of history? And let me tell you this, dear sir. War, in Nature herself outside of man, is so much a rarity that it scarcely exists. In all those two hundred and fifty thousand species, there are only a dozen or so which go to war. If Nature ever troubled to look at man, the little atrocity, she would be shocked out of her wits.

"And finally," concluded the magician, pulling up into a canter, "leaving his morals out of account, is the odious creature important even in a physical sense? Would neutral Nature be compelled to notice him, more than the greenfly or the coral insect, because of the changes which he has effected on the surface of the earth?"

4

THE KING SAID POLITELY, stunned by such a lot of declamation: "Surely she would. Surely we are important from what we have done?"

"How?" demanded his tutor fiercely.

"Well, I must say. Look at the buildings which we have made on the earth, and towns, and arable fields..."

"The Great Barrier Reef," observed Archimedes, looking at the ceiling, "is a building a thousand miles long, and it was built entirely by insects."

"But that is only a reef..."

Merlyn dashed his hat on the floor, in his usual way.

"Can you never learn to think impersonally?" he demanded. "The coral insect would have as much right to reply to you, that London is only a town."

"Even then, if all the towns in the world were placed end to end..."

41

Archimedes said: "If you begin producing all the towns in the world, I shall begin producing all the coral islands and atolls. Then we will weigh them carefully against each other, and we shall see what we shall see."

"Perhaps coral insects are more important than men, then, but this is only one species..."

Goat said slyly: "The committee had a note somewhere about the beaver, I think, in which he was said to have made whole seas and continents...."

"The birds," began Balin with exaggerated nonchalance, "by carrying the seeds of trees in their droppings, are said to have made forests so large..."

"Them rabbits," interrupted the urchin, "whatter nigh deflopulated Austrylia..."

"The Foraminifera of whose bodies the 'white cliffs of Dover' are actually composed..."

"The locusts..."

Merlyn held up his hand.

"Give him the humble earth-worm," he said majestically.

So the animals recited in unison: "The naturalist Darwin has pointed out that there are about 25,000 earth-worms in every field acre, that they turn over in England alone 320,000,000 tons of soil a year, and that they are to be found in almost every region of the world. In thirty years they will alter the whole earth's surface to the depth of seven inches. 'The earth without worms,' says the immortal Gilbert White, 'would soon become cold, hard-bound, void of fermentation, and consequently sterile.'"

5

"IT SEEMS TO ME," said the king happily, for these high matters seemed to be taking him far from Mordred and Lancelot, far from the place where, as they put it in *King Lear*, humanity must perforce prey on itself like monsters of the deep, into the peaceful world where people thought and talked and loved each other without the misery of doing, "it seems to me, if what you say is true, that it would do my fellow humans good to take them down a peg. If they could be taught to look at themselves as another species of mammal for a change, they might find the novelty a tonic. Tell me what conclusions the committee has come to, for I am sure you have been discussing it, about the human animal?"

"We have found ourselves in difficulty about the name."

"What name?"

"Homo sapiens," explained the grass-snake. "It

43

became obvious that *sapiens* was hopeless as an adjective, but the trouble was to find another."

Archimedes said: "Do you remember that Merlyn once told you why the chaffinch was called *coelebs*? A good adjective for a species has to be appropriate to some peculiarity of it, like that."

"The first suggestion," said Merlyn, "was naturally *ferox,* since man is the most ferocious of the animals."

"It is strange that you should mention *ferox.* I was thinking that very word an hour ago. But you are exaggerating, of course, when you say that he is more ferocious than a tiger."

"Am I?"

"I have always found that men were decent on the whole . . ."

Merlyn took off his spectacles, sighed deeply, polished them, put them on again, and examined his disciple with curiosity: as if he might at any moment begin to grow some long, soft, furry ears.

"Try to remember the last time you went for a walk," he suggested mildly.

"A walk?"

"Yes, a walk in the English country lanes. Here comes *Homo sapiens,* taking his pleasure in the cool of the evening. Picture the scene. Here is a blackbird singing in the bush. Does it fall silent and fly away with a curse? Not a bit of it. It sings all the louder and perches on his shoulder. Here is a rabbit nibbling the short grass. Does it rush in terror towards its burrow? Not at all. It hops towards him. Here are field mouse, grass-snake, fox, hedgehog, badger. Do they conceal themselves, or accept his presence?

"Why," cried the old fellow suddenly, flaming out with a peculiar, ancient indignation, "there is not a humble animal in England that does not flee from the shadow of man, as a burnt soul from purgatory. Not a mammal, not a fish, not a bird. Extend your walk so that it passes by a river bank, and the very fish will dart away. It takes something, believe me, to be dreaded in all the elements there are.

"And do not," he added quickly, laying his hand on Arthur's knee, "do not imagine that they fly from the presence of one another. If a fox walked down the lane, perhaps the rabbit would scuttle: but the bird in the tree and the rest of them would agree to his being. If a hawk swung by, perhaps the blackbird would cower: but the fox and the others would allow its arrival. Only man, only the earnest member of the Society for the Invention of Cruelty to Animals, only he is dreaded by every living thing."

"But these animals are not what you could call really wild. A tiger, for instance..."

Merlyn stopped him with his hand again.

"Let the walk be in the Darkest Indies," he said, "if you like. There is not a tiger, not a cobra, not an elephant in the Afric jungle, but what he flies from man. A few tigers who have gone mad from tooth-ache will attack him, and the cobra, if hard pressed, will fight in self-defence. But if a sane man meets a sane tiger on a jungle path, it is the tiger who will turn aside. The only animals which do not run from man are those which have never seen him, the seals, penguins, dodos or whales of the Arctic seas, and these, in consequence, are immediately reduced to the verge of extinction. Even the few creatures which prey on man, the mosquito and the parasitic flea: even these are terrified of their host, and keep a sharp lookout to be beyond his fingers.

"Homo ferox," continued Merlyn, shaking his head, "that rarity in nature, an animal which will kill for pleasure! There is not a beast in this room who would not scorn to kill, except for a meal. Man affects to feel indignation at the shrike, who keeps a small larder of snails etc. speared on thorns: yet his own well-stocked larder is surrounded by herds of charming creatures like the mooning bullock, and the sheep with its intelligent and sensitive face, who are kept solely in order to be slaughtered on the verge of maturity and devoured by their carnivorous herder, whose teeth are not even designed for those of a carnivore. You should read Lamb's letter to Southey, about baking moles alive, and sport with cockchafers, and cats in bladders, and crimping skates, and anglers, those 'meek inflictors of pangs intolerable.' *Homo ferox,* the Inventor of Cruelty to Animals, who will rear pheasants at enormous expense for the pleasure of killing them: who will go to the trouble of training other animals to kill: who will burn living rats, as I have seen done in Eriu, in order that their shrieks may intimidate the local rodents: who will forcibly degenerate the livers of domestic geese, in order to make himself a tasty food: who will saw the growing horns off cattle, for convenience in transport: who will blind goldfinches with a

needle, to make them sing: who will boil lobsters and shrimps alive, although he hears their piping screams: who will turn on his own species in war, and kill nineteen million every hundred years: who will publicly murder his fellow men when he has adjudged them to be criminals: and who has invented a way of torturing his own children with a stick, or of exporting them to concentration camps called Schools, where the torture can be applied by proxy...Yes, you are right to ask whether man can properly be described as *ferox*, for certainly the word in its natural meaning of wild life among decent animals ought never to be applied to such a creature."

"Goodness," said the king. "You seem to lay it on."

But the old magician would not be appeased.

"The reason," he said, "why we felt doubts about using *ferox,* was because Archimedes suggested that *stultus* would be more appropriate."

"*Stultus*? I thought we were intelligent?"

"In one of the miserable wars when I was a younger man," said the magician, taking a deep breath, "it was found necessary to issue to the people of England a set of printed cards which entitled them to food. These cards had to be filled in by hand, before the food could be bought. Each individual had to write a number in one part of the card, his name in another part, and the name of the food-supplier in a third. He had to perform these three intellectual feats—one number and two names—or else he would get no food and starve to death. His life depended on the operation. It was found in the upshot, so far as I recollect, that two thirds of the population were unable to perform the sequence without mistake. And these people, we are told by the Catholic Church, are to be trusted with immortal souls!"

"Are you sure of the facts?" asked the badger doubtfully.

The old man had the grace to blush.

"I did not note them down," he said, "but they are true in substance, if not in detail. I clearly remember, for instance, that a woman was found standing in a queue for bird-seed in the same war, who, upon interrogation, was discovered to possess no birds."

Arthur objected.

"It does not prove very much, even if they were unable to write their three things properly. If they had been any of the other animals, they would not have been able to write at all."

"The short answer to that," replied the philosopher, "is that not a single human being can bore a hole in an acorn with his nose."

"I do not understand."

"Well, the insect called *Balaninus elephas* is able to bore acorns in the way I mention, but it cannot write. Man can write, but cannot bore acorns. These are their own specialisations. The important difference is, however, that while *Balaninus* bores his holes with the greatest efficiency, man, as I have shown you, does not write with any efficiency at all. That is why I say that, species for species, man is more inefficient, more *stultus,* than his fellow beasts. Indeed, no sensible observer would expect the contrary. Man has been so short a time upon our globe, that he can scarcely be expected to have mastered much."

The king had found that he was beginning to feel depressed.

"Did you think of many other names?" he asked.

"There was a third suggestion, made by badger."

At this the happy badger shuffled his feet with satisfaction, peeped sideways at the company round the corner of his spectacles, and examined his long nails.

"*Impoliticus,*" said Merlyn. "*Homo impoliticus.* You remember that Aristotle defined us as political animals. Badger suggested examining this, and, after we had looked at his politics, *impoliticus* seemed to be the only word to use."

"Go on, if you must."

"We found that the political ideas of *Homo ferox* were of two kinds: either that problems could be solved by force, or that they could be solved by argument. The ant-men of the future, who believe in force, consider that you can determine whether twice two is four by knocking people down who disagree with you. The democrats, who are to believe in argument, consider that all men are entitled to an opinion, because all are born equal—'I am as good a man as you are,' the first instinctive ejaculation of the man who is not."

"If neither force nor argument can be relied on," said the king, "I do not see what can be done."

"Neither force, nor argument, nor opinion," said Merlyn with the deepest sincerity, "are *thinking*. Argument is only a display of mental force, a sort of fencing with points in order to gain a victory, not for truth. Opinions are the blind alleys of lazy or of stupid men, who are unable to think. If ever a true politician really thinks a subject out dispassionately, even *Homo stultus* will be compelled to accept his findings in the end. Opinion can never stand beside truth. At present, however, *Homo impoliticus* is content either to argue with opinions or to fight with his fists, instead of waiting for the truth in his head. It will take a million years, before the mass of men can be called political animals."

"What are we, then, at present?"

"We find that at present the human race is divided politically into one wise man, nine knaves, and ninety fools out of every hundred. That is, by an optimistic observer. The nine knaves assemble themselves under the banner of the most knavish among them, and become 'politicians': the wise man stands out, because he knows himself to be hopelessly outnumbered, and devotes himself to poetry, mathematics or philosophy; while the ninety fools plod off behind the banners of the nine villains, according to fancy, into the labyrinths of chicanery, malice and warfare. It is pleasant to have command, observes Sancho Panza, even over a flock of sheep, and that is why the politicians raise their banners. It is, moreover, the same thing for the sheep whatever the banner. If it is democracy, then the nine knaves will become members of parliament; if fascism, they will become party leaders; if communism, commissars. Nothing will be different, except the name. The fools will be still fools, the knaves still leaders, the results still exploitation. As for the wise man, his lot will be much the same under any ideology. Under democracy he will be encouraged to starve to death in a garret, under fascism he will be put in a concentration camp, under communism he will be liquidated. This is an optimistic but on the whole a scientific statement of the habits of *Homo impoliticus*."

The king said grimly: "Well, I am sorry. I suppose I had better go away and drown myself. I am cheeky, insignificant, ferocious, stupid and impolitic. It hardly seems to be worth our going on."

But at this the animals seemed much upset. They rose in a body, stood round him, fanned him, and offered him drink.

"No," they said. "Really, we were not trying to be rude. Honestly, we were trying to help. There, do not take it to heart. We are sure there must be plenty of humans who are *sapiens,* and not a bit ferocious. We were telling you these things as a sort of foundation, so as to make it easier to solve your puzzle later. Come now, have a glass of madeira and think no more about it. Truly, we think that man is the most marvellous creature anywhere, quite the best there is."

And they turned upon Merlyn crossly, saying: "Now look what you have done! This is the result of all your jibber and jabber! The poor king is perfectly miserable, and all because you throw your weight about, and exaggerate, and prattle like a poop!"

Merlyn only replied: "Even the Greek definition *anthropos,* He Who Looks Up, is inaccurate. Man seldom looks above his own height after adolescence."

6

THE NEW ARTHUR, the oiled bolt, was cosseted back to good humour; but he immediately committed the blunder of opening the subject once again.

"Surely," he said, "the affections of men, their love and heroism and patience: surely these are respectable things?"

His tutor was not abashed by the scolding which he had received. He accepted the gage with pleasure.

"Do you suppose that the other animals," he asked, "have no love or heroism or patience—or, which is the more important, no co-operative affection? The love-lives of ravens, the heroism of a pack of weasels, the patience of small birds nursing a cuckoo, the co-operative love of bees—all these things are shewn much more perfectly on every side in nature, than they have ever been shewn in man."

"Surely," asked the king, "man must have some respectable feature?"

At this his magician relented.

"I am inclined to think," he said, "that there may be one. This, insignificant and childish as it must seem, I mention in spite of all the lucubrations of that fellow Chalmers-Mitchell. I refer to man's relation with his pets. In certain households there are dogs which are of no use as hunters or as watchmen, and cats which refuse to go mousing, but which are treated with a kind of vicarious affection by their human fellows, in spite of uselessness or even trouble. I cannot help thinking that any traffic in love, which is platonic and not given in exchange for other commodities, must be remarkable. I knew a donkey once, who lived in the same field with a horse of the same sex. They were deeply attached to one another, although nobody could see that either of them was able to confer a material benefit on the other. This relationship does, it seems to me, exist to a respectable extent between *Homo ferox* and his hounds in certain cases. But it also exists among the ants, so we must not put too much store upon it."

Goat observed slyly: "Parasites."

At this, Cavall got off his master's lap, and he and the new king walked over to the goat on stiff legs. Cavall spoke in human speech for the first and last time in his long life, in unison with his master. His voice sounded like a teuton's speaking through a trumpet.

"Did you say Parasites?" they asked. "Just say

that once again, will you, until we punch your head?"

The goat regarded them with amused affection, but refused to have a row.

"If you punched my head," he said, "you would get a pair of bloody knuckles. Besides, I take it back."

They sat down again, while the king congratulated himself on having something nice in his heart at any rate. Cavall evidently thought the same thing, for he licked his nose.

"What I cannot understand," said Arthur, "is why you should take the trouble to think about man and his problems, or to sit in committee on them, if the only respectable thing about him is

the way he treats a few pets. Why not let him extinguish himself without fuss?"

This set the committee a problem: they remained still to think it over, holding the mahogany fans between their faces and the firelight, and watching the inverted flames in the smoky brown of the madeira.

"It is because we love you, king, yourself," said Archimedes eventually.

This was the most wonderful compliment which he had ever received.

"It is because the creature is young," said the goat. "Young and helpless creatures make you want to aid them, instinctively."

"It is because helping is a good thing anyway," said T. natrix.

"There is something important in humanity," said Balin. "I cannot at present describe it."

Merlyn said: "It is because one likes to tinker with things, to play with possibilities."

The hedgehog gave the best reason, which was simply: "Whoy shouldernt 'un?"

Then they fell silent, musing on the flames.

"Perhaps I have painted a dark picture of the humans," said Merlyn doubtfully, "not very dark, but it might have been a shade lighter. It was because I wanted you to understand about looking at the animals. I did not want you to think that man was too grand to do that. In the course of a long experience of the human race, I have learned that you can never make them understand anything, unless you rub it in."

"You are wanting me to find something out, by learning from the beasts."

"Yes. At last we are getting to the object of your visit. There are two creatures which I forgot to shew you when you were small, and, unless you see them now, we shall get no further."

"I will do what you like."

"They are the Ant and the Wild Goose. We want you to meet them tonight. Of course it will be only one kind of ant, out of many hundreds, but it is a kind which we want you to see."

"Very well," said the king. "I am ready and willing."

"Have you the Sanguinea-spell at hand, my badger?"

The wretched animal immediately began to rummage in its chair, searching inside the seams, lifting the corner of the carpet, and turning up slips of paper covered with Merlyn's handwriting in all directions.

The first slip was headed *More Hubris Under Victoria*. It said: "Dr. John of Gaddesden, court physician to Edward II, claimed to have cured the king's son of small-pox by wrapping the patient up in red cloth, putting red curtains on the windows, and seeing that all the hangings of the room were red. This raised a merry Victorian guffaw at the expense of mediaeval simplicity, until it was discovered by Dr. Niels Finsen of Copenhagen in the twentieth century that red and infra-red light really did affect the pustules of small-pox, even helping in the cure of the disease."

The next slip said briefly: "Half a rose noble each way on Golden Miller."

The third, which smelt strongly of Quelques

Fleurs, and was not in Merlyn's hand, said:
"Queen Philippa's monument at Charing Cross,
seven-thirty, under the spire." There were a lot of
kisses on the bottom of it, and, on the back, some
notes for a poem to be addressed to the sender.
These were in Merlyn's writing, and said: Hooey?
Coué? Chop-suey? The poem itself, which began

Cooee
Nimue,

was erased.

Another slip was headed: *"Other Races,
Victorian Condescension to, as well as to Own
Ancestors, Animals, etc."* It said: "Colonel Wood-
Martin, the Antiquarian, writing in 1895, observes
with a giggle that 'one of the *most-depraved* of all
races, the *now extinct* Tasmanians, believed that

stones, especially certain kinds of quartz crystals, could be used as mediums, or as means of communication... with living persons at a distance!' Within a few years of this note, wireless was imported into the western hemisphere. I prefer to conjecture that these depraved people were a million years in front of the colonel, along the same foul road, and that they had become extinct by constantly listening to swing-music on their crystal sets."

"Here we are," said badger. "I think this is it."

He handed over a strip on which was written: *"Formica est exemplo magni laboris,** Dative of the Purpose."

It proved ineffectual.

At last everybody was commanded to stand up, search on their chairs, look in their pockets, etc. The hedgehog, producing a tattered fragment covered with dry mud and crumbled leaves, on which he had been sitting, asked: "Be 'un thic?" After it had been wiped, flapped and dusted, it was found to read: *Dragguls uoht, Tna eht ot og,* and Merlyn said it was the one they wanted.

So a couple of ants' nests were fetched from the meat-safe, where they stood supported in saucers of water. They were placed on a table in the middle of the room, while the animals sat down to watch, for you could see inside the nests by means of glass plates coloured red. Arthur was made to sit on the table beside the larger nest, the inverted pentagram was drawn, and Merlyn solemnly pronounced the cantrip.

---

*"The ant is an example of great industry."

7

HE FELT THAT it was strange to be visiting the animals again at his age. Perhaps, he thought to himself with shame, I am dreaming in my second childhood, perhaps I am given over to my dotage.

But it made him remember his first childhood vividly, the happy times swimming in moats or flying with Archimedes, and he realised that he had lost something since those days. It was something which he thought of now as the faculty of wonder. Then, his delights had been indiscriminate. His attention, or his sense of beauty, or whatever it was to be called, had attached itself fortuitously to oddments. Perhaps, while Archimedes had been lecturing him about the flight of birds, he himself would have been lost in admiration at the way in which the fur went on the mouse in the owl's claws. Or the great Mr. M. might have been making him a speech about Dictatorship, while he, all the time, would have seen only the bony teeth, poring on them in an ecstasy of experience.

This, his faculty of wonder, was gone from inside him, however much Merlyn might have furbished up his brain. It was exchanged—for the faculty of discrimination, he supposed. Now he would have listened to Archimedes or to Mr. M. He would never have seen the grey fur or the yellow teeth. He did not feel proud of the change.

The old man yawned—for ants do yawn, and they stretch themselves too, just like human beings, when they have had a sleep—after which he gathered his wits for the business in hand. He did not feel pleased to be an ant, as he would have been transported to be one in the old days, but only thought to himself: well, it is a piece of work which I must do. How to begin?

The nests were made by spreading earth in a thin layer, less than half an inch deep, on small tables like footstools. Then, on top of the layer of

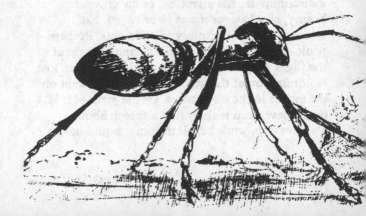

earth, a sheet of glass was placed, with a piece of cloth over it to give darkness for the nurseries. By removing the cloth, you could see into the underground shelters as if you had a cross section. You could see the circular chamber where the pupae were being tended, as if it were a conservatory with a glass roof.

The actual nests were only at the end of the footstools, the glass reaching less than half the way along. In front were plain aprons of earth, open to the sky, and, at the further end of each footstool, there were the watch-glasses in which the syrup was left for food. There was no communication between the two nests. The footstools were separate, side by side but not touching, with their legs in the saucers.

Of course it did not seem like this at the time. The place where he was seemed like a great field of earthen boulders, with a flattened fortress at one end of it. The fortress was entered by tunnels,

and, over the entrance to each tunnel, there was a
notice which said:

EVERYTHING NOT FORBIDDEN IS
COMPULSORY BY NEW ORDER

He read the notice with a feeling of dislike,
though he did not appreciate its meaning, and he
thought to himself: I will take a turn round,
before going in. For some reason the notice gave
him a reluctance to go, making the rough tunnel
look sinister.

He waved his antennae carefully, considering
the notice, assuring himself of his new senses,
planting his feet squarely in the new world as if to
brace himself in it. He cleaned his antennae with
his forefeet, frisking and smoothing them so that
he looked like a Victorian villain twirling his
moustachios. Then he became conscious of
something which had been waiting for
consciousness all the time: that there was a noise
in his head which was articulate. It was either a
noise or a complicated smell, and the easiest way
for us to explain it is to say that it was like a
wireless broadcast. It came to him through his
antennae, like music.

The music had a monotonous rhythm like a
pulse, and the words which went with it were
about June—moon—noon—spoon or Mammy—
mammy—mammy—mammy or Ever—never or
Blue—true—you. He liked them at first, especially
the ones about Love—dove—above, until he
found that they were not variable. As soon as they
had been finished once, they were begun again.

After an hour or two of them, he was to feel that they would make him scream.

There was a voice in his head also, during the pauses of the music, which seemed to be giving directions. "All two-day-olds to be moved to the West Aisle," it would say, or "Number 210397/WD to report to the syrup squad, in replacement of 333105/WD who has fallen off the nest." It was a charming, fruity voice, but seemed to be somehow impersonal: as if the charm were an accomplishment that had been perfected like a circus trick. It was dead.

The king, or perhaps we ought to say the ant, walked away from the fortress as soon as he was prepared to walk about. He began prospecting the desert of boulders uneasily, reluctant to visit the place from which the orders were coming, yet bored with the narrow view. He found small pathways among the boulders, wandering tracks both aimless and purposeful, which led toward the syrup store and also in various other directions which he could not understand. One of these latter paths ended at a clod with a natural hollow underneath it. In the hollow, again with the queer appearance of aimless purpose, he found two dead ants. They were laid there tidily but yet untidily, as if a very tidy person had taken them to the place but forgotten the reason when he got there. They were curled up, and they did not seem to be either glad or sorry to be dead. They were there, like a couple of chairs.

While he was looking at the two corpses, a live ant came down the pathway carrying a third.

It said: "Heil, Sanguinea!"

The king said Hail, politely.

In one respect, of which he knew nothing, he was fortunate. Merlyn had remembered to give him the proper smell for this particular nest; for, if he had smelled of any other nest, they would have killed him at once. If Miss Edith Cavell had been an ant, they would have had to write on her pedestal: SMELL IS NOT ENOUGH.

The new ant put down its cadaver vaguely and began dragging the other two in various directions. It did not seem to know where to put them; or rather, it knew that a certain arrangement had to be made, but it could not figure out how to make it. It was like a man with a tea-cup in one hand and a sandwich in the other, who wants to light a cigarette with a match. But, where the man would invent the idea of putting down the cup and sandwich, before picking up the cigarette and match, this ant would have put down the sandwich and picked up the match, then it would have been down with the match and up with the cigarette, then down with the cigarette and up with the sandwich, then down with the cup and up with the cigarette, until finally it had put down the sandwich and picked up the match. It was inclined to rely upon a series of accidents in order to achieve its objects. It was patient, and did not think. When it had pulled the three dead ants into several positions they would doubtless fall into line under the clod eventually, and that was its whole duty.

The king watched the arrangements with a surprise which turned into vexation and then into dislike. He felt like asking why it did not think things out in advance—that annoyed feeling which one has on seeing a job being badly done. Later he began to wish that he could put several other questions, such as "Do you like being a sexton?" or "Are you a slave?" or even "Are you happy?"

But the extraordinary thing was that he could not ask such questions. In order to ask them, he would have had to put them into the ant language through his antennae: and he now discovered, with a helpless feeling, that there were no words for half the things he wanted to say. There were no words for happiness, for freedom, or for liking, nor were there any words for their opposites. He felt like a dumb man trying to shout "Fire!" The nearest he could get to Right and Wrong, even, was Done or Not-Done.

The ant finished fiddling with its corpses and turned back down the pathway, leaving them in the queer haphazard order. It found that Arthur was in its way, so it stopped, waving its wireless aerials at him as if it were a tank. With its mute, menacing helmet of a face, and its hairiness, and the things like spurs at each leg-joint, perhaps it was more like a knight-in-armour on an armoured horse: or like a combination of the two, a hairy centaur-in-armour.

It said "Heil, Sanguinea" once again.

"Hail."

"What are you doing?"

The king answered truthfully but not wisely: "I am not doing anything."

It was baffled by this for several seconds, as you would be if Einstein were to tell you his latest

ideas about space. Then it extended the twelve joints of its aerial and spoke past him into the blue.

It said: "105978/UDC reporting from square five. There is an insane ant on square five. Over to you."

The word it used for insane was Not-Done. Later on, he was to discover that there were only two qualifications in the language—Done and Not-Done—which applied to all questions of value. If the syrup which Merlyn left for them was sweet, it was a Done syrup: if he had left them some corrosive sublimate, it would have been a Not-Done syrup, and that was that. Even the moons, mammies, doves etc. in the broadcasts were completely described when they were stated to be Done ones.

The broadcast stopped for a moment, and the fruity voice said: "G.H.Q. replying to 105978/UDC. What is its number? Over."

The ant asked: "What is your number?"

"I do not know."

When this news had been exchanged with headquarters, a message came back to ask whether he could give an account of himself. The ant asked him whether he could, using the same words as the broadcaster had used, and in the same flat voice. It made him feel uncomfortable and angry, two emotions which he disliked.

"Yes," he said sarcastically, for it was obvious that the creature could not detect sarcasm, "I have fallen on my head and cannot remember anything about it."

"105978/UDC reporting. Not-Done ant is

suffering from concussion through falling off the nest. Over."

"G.H.Q. replying to 105978/UDC. Not-Done ant is number 42436/WD, who fell off the nest this morning while working with syrup squad. If it is competent to continue its duties—" Competent-to-continue-its-duties was easier in the ant speech, for it was simply Done, like everything else that was not Not-Done: but enough of this language question. "If it is competent to continue its duties, instruct 42436/WD to rejoin syrup squad, relieving 210021/WD, who was sent to replace it. Over."

"Do you understand?" asked the ant.

It seemed that he could not have made a better explanation of himself than this about falling on his head, even if he had meant to; for the ants did occasionally tumble off their footstools, and Merlyn, if he happened to notice them, would lift them back with the end of his pencil.

"Yes."

The sexton paid no further attention to him, but crawled off down the path for another body or for anything else that needed to be scavenged.

Arthur took himelf away in the opposite direction, to join the syrup squad, memorising his own number and the number of the unit who had to be relieved.

8

THE SYRUP SQUAD were standing motionless round
the watch-glass, like a circle of worshippers. He
joined the circle, announcing that 210021/WD was
to return to the nest. Then he began filling himself
with the sweet nectar like the others. At first it
was delicious to him, so that he ate greedily, but
in a few seconds it began to be unsatisfactory: he
could not understand why. He ate hard, copying
the rest of the squad, but it was like eating a
banquet of nothing, or like a dinner-party on the
stage. In a way it was like a nightmare, under
which you might continue to consume huge
masses of putty without being able to stop.

There was a coming and going round the
watch-glass. Those ants who had filled their crops
to the brim were walking back to the fortress, to
be replaced by a procession of empty ants who
were coming from the same direction. There were
never any new ants in the procession, but only this

same dozen going backwards and forwards, as they would do during all their lives.

He realized suddenly that what he was eating was not going into his stomach. Only a tiny proportion of it had penetrated to his private self at the beginning, and now the main mass was being stored in a kind of upper stomach or crop, from which it could be removed. It dawned on him at the same time that when he joined the westward stream he would have to disgorge this store, into a larder or something of that sort.

The sugar squad conversed with each other while they worked. He thought this was a good sign at first, and listened, to pick up what he could.

"Oh hark!" one of them would say. "Here comes that Mammy—mammy—mammy— mammy song again. I do think that Mammy—

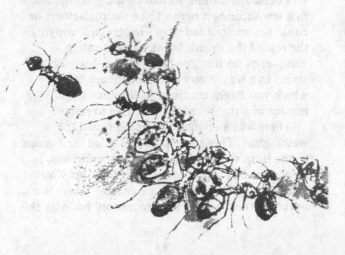

mammy—mammy—mammy song is loverly
(Done). It is so high-class (Done)."

Another would remark: "I do think our
beloved Leader is wonderful, do not you? They
say she was stung three hundred times in the last
war, and was awarded the Ant Cross for Valour."

"How lucky we are to be born of the Sanguinea
blood, don't you think, and would it not be awful
to be one of those filthy *Formicae fuscae!*"

"Was it not awful about 310099/WD, who
refused to disgorge his syrup when he was asked.
Of course he was executed at once, by special
order of our beloved Leader."

"Oh hark! Here comes that Mammy—
mammy—mammy—mammy song again. I do
think..."

He walked off to the nest with a full gorge,
leaving them to do the round again. For they had
no news, no scandal, nothing to talk about.
Novelties did not happen to them. Even the
remarks about the executions were in a formula,
and only varied as to the registration number of
the criminal. When they had finished with the
Mammy—mammy—mammy—mammy, they had
to go on to the beloved Leader and then to the
filthy *fuscae* and to the latest execution. It went
round in a circle. Even the beloveds, wonderfuls,
luckies and so on were all Dones, and the awfuls
were Not-Dones.

He found himself in the vast hall of the
fortress, where hundreds and hundreds of ants
were licking or feeding in the nurseries, carrying
grubs to various aisles in order to get an even
temperature, and opening or closing the

ventilation passages. In the middle, the giant Leader sat complacently, laying eggs, attending to the broadcasts, issuing directions or commanding executions, surrounded by a sea of adulation. (He learned later from Merlyn that the method of succession among these Leaders was variable according to the different species of ant. In *Bothriomyrmex,* for instance, the ambitious founder of a New Order would invade a nest of *Tapinoma* and jump upon the back of the older tyrant: there, dissimulated by the smell of her host, she would slowly saw off her head, until she herself had achieved the right of leadership.)

There was no larder for his store of syrup after all. He found that he must walk about like a living dumb-waiter at the convenience of the indoor workers. When they wanted a meal, they stopped him, he opened his mouth, and they fed from it. They did not treat him as a person, and, indeed, they were impersonal themselves. He was a dumb-waiter from which dumb-diners fed. Even his stomach was not his own.

But do not let us go on about these ants in too much detail: they are not a pleasant topic. He lived among them patiently, conforming to their habits, watching them in order to understand as much as possible, but unable to ask them questions. It was not only that their language was destitute of the words in which he was interested, so that it was impossible to ask them whether they believed in Life, Liberty and the Pursuit of Happiness, but also that it was dangerous to ask them questions at all. A question was a sign of insanity to them, because their life was not

questionable: it was dictated. He crawled from
nest to syrup and back again, exclaimed that the
Mammy song was loverly, opened his jaws to
regurgitate, and tried to understand as well as he
could.

He had reached the screaming stage when the
enormous hand came down from the clouds,
carrying a straw. It placed the straw between the
two nests, which had been separate before, so that
now there was a bridge between them. Then it
went away.

9

LATER IN THE DAY a black ant came wandering
over the new bridge: one of the wretched *fuscae*, a
humble race who would only fight in self-defence
It was met by one of the scavengers and
murdered.

The broadcasts changed after this news had
been reported, as soon as it had been established
by spies that the *fusca* nest had also its glass of
syrup.

Mammy—mammy—mammy gave place to
Antland, Antland Over All, while the stream of
orders were discontinued in favour of lectures
about war, patriotism and the economic situation.
The fruity voice announced that their beloved
country was being encircled by a horde of filthy
fuscae—at which the wireless chorus sang

> When fusca *blood spurts from the knife,*
> Then everything is fine—

and it also explained that Ant the Father had ordained in his inscrutable wisdom that black pismires should always be the slaves of red ones. Their beloved country had no slaves at present, a disgraceful state of affairs which would have to be remedied if the master race were not to perish. A third statement was that the national property of Sanguinea was being threatened: their syrup was to be stolen, their domestic animals, the beetles, were to be kidnapped, and their communal stomach would be starved. The king listened to two of these talks carefully, so that he was able to remember them afterwards.

The first one was arranged as follows:

A. *We are so numerous that we are starving.*

B. *Therefore we must not cut down our numbers but encourage large families in order to become still more numerous and starving.*

C. *When we are so numerous and starving as all that, obviously we have a right to take other people's syrup. Besides, we shall by then have a numerous and starving army.*

It was only after this logical train of thought had been put into practise, and the output of the nurseries trebled—Merlyn meanwhile giving them ample syrup daily for all their needs: for it has to be admitted that starving nations never seem to be quite so poor that they cannot afford to have far more expensive armaments than anybody else—that the second type of lecture was commenced.

This is how the second kind went:

A. *We are more numerous than they are, therefore we have a right to their syrup.*

B. *They are more numerous than we are, therefore they are wickedly trying to steal our syrup.*

C. We are a mighty race and have a natural right
    to subjugate their puny one.

D. They are a mighty race and are unnaturally
    trying to subjugate our inoffensive one.

E. We must attack in self-defence.

F. They are attacking us by defending
    themselves.

G. If we do not attack them today, they will
    attack us tomorrow.

H. In any case we are not attacking them at all:
    we are offering them incalculable benefits.

After the second type of address, the religious
services began. These dated, he discovered, from a
fabulous past so ancient that he could scarcely
find a date for it, in which the emmets had not yet
settled down to socialism. They came from a time
when ants were still like men, and terribly
impressive some of them were.

A psalm at one of these services, beginning, if
we allow for the difference of language, with the
well-known words, "the earth is the Sword's and
all that therein is, the compass of the bomber and
they that bomb therefrom," ended with the terrific
conclusion: "Blow up your heads, O ye Gates, and
be ye blown up, ye Everlasting Doors, that the
King of Tories may come in. Who is the King of
Tories? Even the Lord of Ghosts, He is the King
of Tories."

A strange feature was that the common ants

were neither exalted by the songs nor interested by the lectures. They accepted them as matters of course. They were rituals to them, like the Mammy songs or the conversations about their beloved Leader. They did not regard these things as good or bad, exciting, rational or terrible: they did not regard them at all, but accepted them as Done.

Well, the time came for the slave war. All the preparations were in order, all the soldiers were drilled to the last ounce, all the walls of the nest carried patriotic slogans such as *Stings or Syrup?* or *I Vow to Thee, my Smell,* and the king was past hoping. He thought he had never been among such horrible creatures, unless it were at the time when he had lived among men, and he was beginning to sicken with disgust. The repetitive voices in his head, which he could not shut off: the absence of all privacy, under which others ate from his stomach while others again sang in his brain: the dreary blank which replaced feeling: the dearth of all but two values: the monotony more even than the callous wickedness: these had killed the joy of life which had been Merlyn's gift at the beginning of the evening. He was as miserable again as he had been when the magician found him weeping at his papers, and now, when the Red Army marched to war at last, he suddenly faced about in the middle of the straw like an insane creature, ready to oppose their passage with his life.

10

"DEAR GOD," said Merlyn, who was patting the beads of sweat on his forehead with a handkerchief, "you certainly have a flair for getting into trouble. That was a difficult minute."

The animals looked at him anxiously, to see if any bones were broken.

"Are you safe?"

"Perfectly."

They discovered that he was furiously angry. His hands were trembling with rage.

"The brutes!" he exclaimed. "The brutes!"

"They are not attractive."

"I would not have minded," he burst out, "if they had been wicked—if they had wanted to be wicked. I would not have minded if they had chosen to be wicked for some reason, or for fun. But they did not know, they had not chosen. They—they—they did not exist!"

"Sit down," said the badger, "and have some rest."

"The horrible creatures! It was like talking to minerals which could move, like talking to statues or to machines. If you said something which was not suitable to the mechanism, then it worked: if not, it did not work, it stood still, it was blank, it had no expression. Oh, Merlyn, how hideous! They were the walking dead. When did they die? Did they ever have any feelings? They have none now. They were like that door in the fairy story, which opened when you said Sesame. I believe that they only knew about a dozen words, or collections of words. A man with those in his mind could have made them do all the things they could do, and then... Then you would have had to start again! Again and again and again! It was like being in Hell. Except that none of them knew they were there. None of them knew anything. Is there anything more terrible than perpetual motion, than doing and doing and doing, without a reason, without a consciousness, without a change, without an end?"

"Ants *are* Perpetual Motion," said Merlyn, "I suppose. I never thought of that."

"The most dreadful thing about them was that they were like human beings—not human, but like humans, a bad copy."

"There is nothing surprising in that. The ants adopted the line of politics which man is flirting with at present, in the infinite past. They perfected it thirty million years ago, so that no further development was possible, and, since then, they have been stationary. Evolution ended with the ants some 30,000,000 years before the birth of Christ. They are the perfect communist state."

Here Merlyn raised his eyes devoutly to the ceiling, and remarked: "My old friend Marx may have been a first-rate economist; but, Holy Ghost, he was a by-our-lady rotten hand at natural history."

Badger, who always took the kindly view of everybody, even of Karl Marx, whose arrangement of his materials was about as lucid as the badger's, by the way, said: "Surely that is hardly fair to actual communism? I would have thought that ants were more like Mordred's fascists than John Ball's communists . . ."

"The one is a stage of the other. In perfection they are the same."

"But in a proper communist world . . ."

"Give the king some wine," said Merlyn. "Urchin, what on earth are you thinking about?"

The hedgehog scuttled off for the decanter, and brought it with a glass. He thrust a moist nose against the king's ear, breathed heavily into it with a breath that smelt of onions, and whispered hoarsely: "Us wor a watchin of 'ee, us wor. Trust tiggy. Tha woulder beat 'em, tha 'ood. Mollocky beästs." Here he nodded his head repeatedly, spilled the madeira, and made boxing movements against the air with the decanter in one hand and the glass in the other. "Free cheers for his Maggy's tea, ez wot us says, that's wot us says. Let un get at 'em, us says, for to lay darn me life with the Shire. And us woulder done, that us 'ood, bim-bam, only for they wouldernt let 'un."

Badger did not wish to be cheated of his defence. He began again patiently as soon as the king was served.

"The ants fight wars," he said, "so they cannot be communists. In a proper communist world there would be no war, because the whole world would be a union. You must not forget that communism has not been properly achieved until all the nations in the world are communistic, and fused together in a *Union* of socialist soviet republics. Now the ant-hills are not fused with one another into a union, so they are not fully communistic, and that is why they fight."

"They are not united," said Merlyn crossly, "only because the smallness of the ant-hills compared with the bigness of the world, and of the natural obstacles such as rivers and so forth, makes communication impossible for animals of their size and number of fingers. Still, if you like, I will agree that they are perfect Thrashers,

prevented from developing into perfect Lollards by geographic and physical features."

"You must therefore withdraw your criticism of Karl Marx."

"Withdraw my criticism?" exclaimed the philosopher.

"Yes; for Marx did solve the king's puzzle of war, by his *Union* of S.S.R."

Merlyn became blue in the face, bit off a large piece of his beard, pulled out tufts of his hair and threw them in the air, prayed fervently for guidance, sat down beside the badger, and, taking him by the hand, looked beseechingly into his spectacles.

"But do you not see," he asked pathetically, "that a union of *anything* will solve the problem of war? You cannot have war in a union, because there must be a division before you can begin one. There would be no war if the world consisted of a union of mutton chops. But this does not mean that we must all rush off and become a series of mutton chops."

"In fact," said the badger, after pondering for some time, "you are not defining the ants as fascists or communists because they fight wars, but because..."

"I am lumping all three sects together on their basic assumption, which is, ultimately, to deny the rights of the individual."

"I see."

"Theirs is the totalitarian theory: that men or ants exist for the sake of the state or world, not vice versa."

"And why did you say that Marx was bad at natural history?"

"The character of my old friend Karl," said the magician severely, "is outside the province of this committee. Kindly remember that we are not sitting on communism, but on the problem of organised murder. It is only in so far as communism is contingent with war, that we are concerned with him at all. With this proviso I reply to your question as follows: that Marx was a bad naturalist because he committed the gross blunder of over-looking the human skull in the first place, because he never considered the geese, and because he subscribed to the Égalité Fallacy, which is abhorrent to nature. Human beings are no more equal in their merits and abilities, than they are equal in face and stature. You might just as well insist that all the people in the world should wear the same size of boot. This ridiculous idea of equality was adopted by the ants more than 30,000,000 years ago, and, by believing it all that time, they have managed to make it true. Now look what a mess they are in."

"Liberty, Equality and Fraternity..." began the badger.

"Liberty, Brutality and Obscenity," rejoined the magician promptly. "You should try living in some of the revolutions which use that slogan. First they proclaim it: then they announce that the aristos must be liquidated, on high moral grounds, in order to purge the party or to prune the commune or to make the world safe for democracy; and then they rape and murder everybody they can lay their hands on, more in sorrow than in anger, or crucify them, or torture them in ways which I do not care to mention. You should have tried the Spanish Civil War. Yes, that is the equality of man. Slaughter anybody who is better than you are, and then we shall be equal soon enough. All equally dead."

11

T. NATRIX SPOKE UP SUDDENLY.

"You humans," he said, "have no idea of the eternity which you prattle about, with your souls and purgatories and so on. If any of you really did believe in Eternity, or even in very long stretches of Time, you would think twice about equality. I can imagine nothing more terrifying than an Eternity filled with men who were all the same. The only thing which has made life bearable in the long past, has been the diversity of creatures on the surface of the globe. If we had all been equal, all one sort of creature, we should have begged for euthanasia long ago. Fortunately there is no such thing in nature as equality of ability, merit, opportunity, or reward. Every species of animal which is still alive—we leave aside the things like ants—is intensely individualistic, thanks be to God. Otherwise we should die of boredom, or become automatons. Even sticklebacks, which, on a first inspection, you would think were pretty much the same as one another: even sticklebacks have geniuses and dunces, all competing for the morsel of food, and it is the geniuses who get it. There was a man who always fed his sticklebacks by putting a glass jar into the aquarium, with the food inside it. Some of them found the way in after three or four attempts, and remembered it, while others, so far as I know or care, are trying still. If this were not so, Eternity would be too terrible to contemplate, because it would be devoid of difference, and therefore change."

"None of this is in order. We are supposed to be considering war."

"Very well."

"King," asked the magician, "can you face the geese yet, or do you want a rest?"

"It is impossible," he added in parentheses, "to consider the subject sensibly, until he has the facts."

The old man said: "I think I must rest. I am not so young as I was, in spite of your massage, and you have been asking me to learn a great many things, in little time. Can you spare a few short minutes?"

"Certainly. The nights are long. Urchin, dip this handkerchief in vinegar and put it on his head. There, put your feet on a chair and close your eyes. Now then, everybody is to keep quite quiet and give him air."

So the animals sat as still as mice, nudging each other when they coughed, and the king, with closed eyes and a sense of thankfulness, slipped into his own thoughts.

For they had been pressing hard. It was difficult to learn it in one night, and he was only human, as well as old.

Perhaps, after all, the careworn person who had been brought from the tent at Salisbury ought never to have been Merlyn's choice. He had been an undistinguished child, although he had been a loving one, and he was far from being a genius still. Perhaps, after all, the whole of our long story has been about a rather dim old gentleman, who would have been better off at Cranford or at Badger's Green, arranging for the village cricket and the choir treat.

There was a thing which he had been wanting to think about. His face, with the hooded eyes, ceased to be like the boy's of long ago. He looked tired, and was the king: which made the others watch him seriously, with fear and sorrow.

They were good and kind, he knew. They were people whose respect he valued. But their problem was not the human one. It was well for them, who had solved their social questions before his men were ever on earth, to consider wisely in their happy College of Life. Their benevolence, with wine and firelight and security towards each other, was easier for them than his sad work for him, their tool.

The old king's eyes being shut, he slid back into the real world from which he had come, his wife abducted, his best friend banished, his nephews slain, his son at his throat. The worst was the impersonal: that all his fellow beings were in it. It was true indeed that man was ferocious, as the animals had said. They could say it abstractly, even with a certain dialectic glee, but for him it was the concrete: it was for him to live among yahoos in flesh and blood. He was one of them himself, cruel and silly like them, and bound to them by the strange continuum of human consciousness. He was an Englishman, and England was at war. However much he hated it, or willed to stop it, he was lapped round in a real but intangible sea of English feeling which he could not control. To go against it, to wrestle with the sea, was more than he could face again.

And he had been working all his life. He knew he was not a clever man. Goaded by the conscience of that old scientist who had fastened on his soul in youth, hag-ridden and devoured, burdened like Sinbad, stolen away from himself and claimed remorselessly for abstract service, he had toiled for Gramarye since before he could remember. He had not even understood the whole of what he was doing, a beast of burden tugging at the traces. And always, he now saw, Merlyn had been behind him—that very ruthless old believer—and man in front: ferocious, stupid, unpolitical.

They wanted him, he now saw, to go back to the labour: to do it worse, and more. Just when he had given up, just when he had been weeping and defeated, just when the old ox had dropped in the traces, they had come again to prick him to his feet. They had come to teach a further lesson, and to send him on.

But he had never had a happiness of his own, never had himself: never since he was a little boy in the Forest Sauvage. It was not fair to steal

away everything from him. They had made him
like the blinded gold-finch they were speaking of,
which was to pour out its song for man until it
burst its heart, but always blind.

He felt, now that they had made him younger,
the intense beauty of the world which they denied
him. He wanted to have some life; to lie upon the
earth, and smell it: to look up into the sky like
anthropos, and lose himself in the clouds. He
knew suddenly that nobody, living upon the
remotest, most barren crag in the ocean, could
complain of a dull landscape so long as he would
lift his eyes. In the sky there was a new landscape
every minute, in every pool of the sea rocks, a new
world. He wanted time off, to live. He did not
want to be sent back to pull, with lowered eyes, at
the weary yoke. He was not quite old even now.
Perhaps he would be able to live for another ten
years—but years in the sunlight, years without
loads, years with the birds singing as they did sing
still, no doubt, although he had ceased to notice
them until the animals reminded him.

Why must he go back to *Homo ferox,*
probably to be killed by those he was trying to
help, certainly, if not, to die in harness, when he
could abdicate the labour? He could walk out
now, straight from the tumulus, and be seen no
more. The monks of the Thebaid, the early saints
on Skellig Michael: these fortunate people had
escaped from man, into a nature which was
surrounded by peace. And that was what he
wanted, he discovered, more than anything else—
only Peace. Earlier in the evening he had wanted
death, and had been ready to accept it: but now

they had given him a glimpse of life, of the old happiness and of the things he had loved. They had revived, how cruelly, his boyhood. He wanted to be let alone, to be off duty like a boy, to retire perhaps into a cloister, to have tranquility for his own old heart.

But they woke him with words, their cruel, bright weapons.

"Now then, king. We must see to these geese, or the night will be over."

"Do you feel better?"

"Has anybody seen the cantrip?"

"You are looking tired."

"Have a sip of wine before you go."

12

THE PLACE WHERE HE WAS, was absolutely flat. In
the human world we seldom see flatness, for the
trees and houses and hedges give a serrated edge
to the landscape: even the grass sticks up with its
myriad blades. But here, in the belly of the night,
the illimitable, flat, wet mud was as featureless as
a dark junket. If it had been wet sand, even, it
would have had those little wave marks, like the
palate of one's mouth.

And, in this enormous flatness, there lived one
element: the wind. For it was an element; it was a
dimension, a power of darkness. In the human
world, the wind comes from somewhere, and goes
somewhere, and, as it goes, it passes through
somewhere: through trees or streets or hedgerows.
This wind came from nowhere. It was going
through the flatness of nowhere, to no place.
Horizontal, soundless except for a peculiar boom,
tangible, infinite, the astounding dimensional

weight of it streamed across the mud. You could have ruled it with a straight-edge. The titanic grey line of it was unwavering and solid. You could have hooked the crook of your umbrella over it, and it would have hung there.

The king, facing into this wind, felt that he was uncreated. Except for the wet solidity under his webbed feet, he was living in nothing: a solid nothing, like chaos. His were the feelings of a point in geometry, existing mysteriously on the shortest distance between two points: or of a line, drawn on a plane surface which had length, breadth but no magnitude. No magnitude! It was the very self of magnitude. It was power, current, force, direction, a pulseless world-stream steady in limbo.

Bounds had been set to this unhallowed purgatory. Far away to the east, perhaps a mile distant, there was an unbroken wall of sound. It surged a little, seeming to expand and contract, but it was solid. It was menacing, being desirous for victims: for it was the huge, the remorseless sea.

Two miles to the west, there were three spots of light in a triangle. They were the weak wicks from fishermen's cottages, who had risen early to catch a tide in the complicated creeks of the salt marsh. Its waters sometimes ran contrary to the ocean. These were the total features of his world, the sea sound and the three small lights: darkness, flatness, vastness, wetness: and, in the gulf of the night, the gulf-stream of the wind.

When daylight began to come, by premonition, he found that he was standing among a crowd of people like himself. They were seated on the mud, which now began to be disturbed by the angry, thin, returning sea, or else were already riding on the water, wakened by it, outside the annoyance of the surf. The seated ones were large teapots, their spouts tucked under their wings. The swimming ones occasionally ducked their heads and shook them. Some, waking on the mud, stood up and wagged their wings vigourously. Their profound silence became broken by a conversational gabble. There were about four hundred of them in the grey vicinity: very beautiful creatures, the wild White-Fronted Geese, whom, once a man has seen them, he will never forget.

Long before the sun came, they were making ready for their flight. Family parties of the previous year's breeding were coming together in batches, and these batches were themselves inclined to join up with other ones, possibly under the command of a grandfather, or of a great-grandfather, or else of some noted leader in the host. When the drafts were complete, there came a faint tone of excitement into their speech. They began moving their heads from side to side in jerks. And then, turning into the wind, suddenly they would all be in the air together, fourteen or forty at a time, with wide wings scooping the blackness and a cry of triumph in their throats. They would wheel round, climbing rapidly, and be gone from sight. Twenty yards up, they were invisible in the dark. The earlier departures were not vocal: they were inclined to be taciturn before the sun came, only making occasional remarks, or crying their single warning-note if danger threatened. Then, at the warning, they would all rise vertically to the sky.

He began to feel an uneasiness in himself. The dim squadrons about him, setting out minute by minute, infected him with a tendency. He became restless to embrace their example, but he was shy. Perhaps their family groups, he thought, would resent his intrusion: yet he wanted not to be lonely: he wanted to join in, and to enjoy the exercise of morning flight, which was so evidently a pleasure to them. They had a comradeship, a free discipline and a joie-de-vivre.

When the goose next to him spread her wings and leaped, he did so automatically. Some eight of those nearby had been jerking their bills, which he had imitated as if the act were catching, and now, with these same eight, he found himself on pinion in the horizontal air. The moment he had left the earth, the wind had vanished: its restlessness and brutality had dropped away as if cut off by a knife: he was in it, and at peace.

The eight geese spread out in line astern, evenly spaced, with him behind. They made for the east, where the poor lights had been, and now, before them, the bold sun began to rise. A crack of orange broke the black cloud-bank far beyond the land; the glory spread, the salt marsh growing visible below. He saw it like a featureless moor or bogland, which had become maritime by accident; its heather, still looking like heather, having mated with the seaweed until it was a salt wet heather, with slippery fronds. The burns which should have run through the moorland were of sea-water on blueish mud. There were long nets here and there, erected on poles, into which unwary geese might fly. These, he now guessed, had been the occasions of those warning-notes. Two or three widgeon hung in one of them, and, far away to the eastward, a fly-like man was plodding over the slob in tiny persistence, to collect his bag.

The sun, as it rose, tinged the quicksilver of the creeks and the gleaming slime itself with flame. The curlew, who had been piping their mournful plaints since long before the light, flew now from weed-bank to weed-bank: the widgeon, who had slept on water, came whistling their double notes, like whistles from a Christmas cracker: the mallard toiled from land, against the wind: the redshanks scuttled and prodded like mice: a cloud of tiny dunlin, more compact than starlings, turned in the air with the noise of a train: the black-guard of crows rose from the pine trees on the dunes with merry cheers: shore birds of every sort populated the tide line, filling it with business and beauty.

The dawn, the sea-dawn and the mastery of ordered flight, were of such intense beauty that he was almost moved to sing. All the sorrow of his thoughts about man, the miserable wishes for peace which had beset him in the Combination Room so lately, these fell from him for the moment in the glory of his wings. He would have liked to cry a chorus to life, and, since a thousand geese were on the wing about him, he had not long to wait. The lines of these creatures, wavering like smoke upon the sky as they breasted the sunrise, were all at once in music and in laughter. Each squadron of them was in different voice, some larking, some triumphant, some in sentiment or glee. The vault of daybreak filled itself with heralds, and this is what they sang:

Oh, turning world, pouring beneath our
 pinions.
Hoist the hoar sun to welcome morning's
 minions.

See, on each breast the scarlet and vermillion,
Hear, from each throat the clarion and
 carillion.

Mark, the wild wandering lines in black
 battalions,
Heaven's horns and hunters, dawn-bright
 hounds and stallions.

Free, free: far, far: and fair on wavering wings
Comes Anser albifrons, and sounds, and
 sings.

13

HE FOUND HIMSELF in a coarse field, in daylight.
His companions of the flight were grazing round
him, plucking the grass with sideways wrenches of
their soft bills, bending their necks into abrupt
loops, unlike the graceful curves of the swan.
Always, as they fed, one of their number was on
guard, its head erect and snakelike. They had
mated during the winter months, or else in
previous winters, so that they tended to feed in
pairs within the family and squadron. The young
female, his neighbour of the mud-flats, was
unmated. She kept an intelligent eye upon him.

The old man who had remembered his
boyhood, watching her secretly, could not help
thinking she was beautiful. He even felt a
tenderness towards her downy breast, as yet quite
innocent of bars; towards her plump compacted
frame and the neat furrows of her neck. These
furrows, he saw out of the corner of his eye, were

caused by a difference in the feathering. The feathers were concave, which separated them from one another, making a texture of ridges which he considered graceful.

Presently the young woman gave him a shove with her bill. She had been acting sentry.

"Go on," she said vulgarly. "You next."

She lowered her head without waiting for an answer, and began to graze in the same manner. Her feeding took her from his side.

He stood as sentry. He did not know what he was watching, nor could he see any enemy, except the tussocks and his nibbling mates; but he was not sorry to be a trusted sentinel. He was surprised to find that he was not averse to seeming masculine, in case the lady might be watching. He was still too innocent, after all his years, to know that she would certainly be doing so.

"What ever are you doing?" she asked, passing him after half an hour.

"I was on guard."

"Go on with you," she said with a giggle, or should it be a gaggle? "You are a silly one."

"Why?"

"Go on. You know."

"Honestly," he said, "I do not. Am I doing it wrong? I not understand."

"Peck the next one. You have been on for twice your time, at least."

He did as he was bid, at which the grazer next to him took over, and then he walked along to feed beside her. They nibbled, noting each other out of beady eyes, until he came to a decision.

"You think I am stupid," he said awkwardly, confessing the secret of his species for the first time in a varied intercourse with animals, "but it is because I am not a goose. I was born a human. This is my first flight among the grey people."

She was only mildly surprised.

"It is unusual," she said. "The humans generally try the swans. The last lot we had were the Children of Lir. However, I suppose we are all Anseriformes together."

"I have heard of the Children of Lir."

"They did not enjoy it. They were hopelessly nationalistic and religious, which resulted in their always hanging about round one of the chapels in Ireland. You could say that they hardly noticed the other swans at all."

"I am enjoying it," he said politely.

"I noticed you were. What were you sent for?"

"To learn about the world."

They grazed away in silence, until his own words reminded him of his mission.

"The sentries," he enquired. "Are we at war?"

She did not understand.

"War?"

"Are we fighting against people?"

"Fighting?" she asked doubtfully. "The men fight sometimes, about their wives and that. Of course there is no bloodshed, only scuffling to find the better man. Is that what you mean?"

"No. I meant fighting against armies: against other geese, for instance."

She was amused at this.

"How ridiculous! You mean a lot of geese all

scuffling at the same time. It would be amusing to watch."

Her tone surprised him.

"Amusing to watch them kill each other!"

"To kill each other? An army of geese to kill each other?"

She began to understand the idea very slowly and doubtfully, an expression of grief and distaste coming over her face. When it had sunk in, she left him. She went away to another part of the field in silence. He followed her, but she turned her back. Moving round to get a glimpse of her eyes, he was startled by their abhorrence: a look as if he had made an obscene suggestion.

He said lamely: "I am sorry. You do not understand."

"Leave talking about it."

"I am sorry."

Later he added: "A person can ask, I suppose. It seems a natural question, with the sentries."

But she was thoroughly angry, almost tearful.

"Will you stop about it at once! What a horrible mind you must have! You have no right to say such things. And of course there are sentries. There are the jerfalcons and the peregrines, are there not: the foxes and the ermines and the humans with their nets? These are natural enemies. But what creature could be so low and treacherous as to murder the people of its blood?"

He thought: it is a pity that there are no big creatures to prey on humanity. If there were enough dragons and rocs, perhaps mankind would turn its might against them. Unfortunately man is preyed upon by microbes, which are too small to be appreciated.

Out loud, he said: "I was trying to learn."

She relented with an obvious effort to be good-natured. She wanted to be broad-minded if she could, as she was rather a blue-stocking.

"You have a long way to go."

"Then you must teach me. You must tell me about the goose-people, so that I improve my mind."

She was doubtful, after the shock which he had given her, but her heart was not a malicious one. Like all the geese, she had a mildness which found forgiving easy. Soon they were friends.

"What would you like to know?"

He discovered, in the next few days, for they spent much time together, that Lyó-lyok was a charming person. She had told him her name at the beginning of their acquaintance, and had advised him to have one of his own. They had chosen Kee-kwa, a distinguished title taken from the rare red-breasted geese whom she had met in Siberia. Afterwards, once they were on name terms, she had buckled to his education manfully.

Lyó-lyok's mind did not run upon flirtation only. She took a rational interest in the wide world in her prudent way, and, although she was puzzled by his questions, she learned not to be disgusted by them. Most of these questions were based on his experience among the ants, and that was why they puzzled her.

He wanted to know about nationalism, about

state-control, individual liberty, property and so forth: the things whose importance had been mentioned in the Combination Room, or which he had noticed in the ant-hill. As most of these things had to be explained to her, before she could explain herself, there were interesting things to talk about. They conversed amiably, and, as his education prospered, the surprised old man began to feel a sort of deep humility and even an affection for her geese: rather like the feelings which Gulliver must have had, among the horses.

No, she explained to him: there was no state-control among the grey people. They had no communal possessions, nor did they make a claim to any part of the world. The lovely globe, they thought, could not belong to anybody except itself, and all their geese had access to its raw materials. Neither was any state discipline imposed upon the individual bird. The story of how a returning ant could be sentenced to death if it did not disgorge some food when asked for it, revolted her. Among the geese, she said, everybody ate as much as he could get hold of, and, if you trespassed upon an individual who had found a succulent patch of grass, he would very properly peck you soundly. And yes, she said, they did have private property besides their meals: a married couple would repair to the same nest, year by year, although they might have travelled many thousand miles between. The nest was private, and so was family life. Geese, she explained, were not promiscuous in their love-affairs, except in adolescence; which, she believed, was as it should be. When they were married, they were married for their lives. Their politics, so far as they had any, were patriarchal or individualistic, founded on free choice. And of course they never went to war.

He asked her about the system of leadership. It was obvious that certain geese were accepted as leaders—generally they were venerable old gentlemen whose breasts were deeply mottled—and that these leaders flew at the head of their formations. Remembering the queen ants, who, like Borgias, slew one another for the highest place, he wondered how the captains of the geese had been elected.

They were not elected, she said, not in a formal way. They simply became captains.

When he pressed her on the point, she went off into a long talk about migration. This was how she put it. "The first goose," she said, "I suppose, who made the flight from Siberia to Lincolnshire and back again, must have brought up a family in Siberia. Then, when the winter came upon them and it was necessary to find new food, he must have groped his way over the same route, being the only one who knew it. He will have been followed by his growing family, year after year, their pilot and their admiral. When the time came for him to die, obviously the next best pilots would have been his eldest sons, who would have covered the route more often than the others. Naturally the younger sons and fledgelings would have been uncertain about it, and therefore would have been glad to follow someone who knew. Perhaps, among the eldest sons, there would have been some who were notoriously muddleheaded, and the family would hardly care to trust to them.

"This," she said, "is how an admiral is elected. Perhaps Wink-wink will come to our family in the autumn, and he will say: 'Excuse me, but have you by any chance got a reliable pilot in your lot? Poor grand-dad died at cloud-berry time, and Uncle Onk is inefficient. We were looking for somebody to follow.' Then we will say: 'Great-uncle will be delighted if you care to hitch up with us; but mind, we cannot take responsibility if things go wrong.' 'Thank you very much,' he will say. 'I am sure your great-uncle can be relied upon. Do you mind if I mention this matter to the Honks, who are, I happen to know, in the same difficulty?' 'Not at all.'

"And that," she explained, "is how great-uncle became an admiral."

"It seems an excellent way."

"Look at his bars," she said respectfully, and they both glanced at the portly patriarch, whose breast was indeed barred with black stripes, like the gold rings on an admiral's sleeve.

On another occasion, he asked about the joys and ambitions of the geese. He told her apologetically that among the human beings a life without spectacular acquisitions, or even without warfare, might tend to be regarded as tedious.

"Humans," he said, "make for themselves great stores of ornaments, riches, luxuries, pleasures and so forth. This gives them an objective in their lives. It is also said to lead to war. But I fear that if they were reduced to the minimum of possessions, with which you geese are contented, they might be unhappy."

"They certainly would be. Their brains are differently shaped from ours. If you tried to make the humans live exactly like the geese, they would be as wretched as the geese would be, if you tried to make them live exactly like the humans. That does not mean that one of them cannot learn a little from the other."

"I am beginning to think that the geese cannot learn very much from us."

"We have been on the earth for millions of years longer than you have, poor creatures, so you can hardly be blamed."

"But tell me," he said, "about your pleasures, your ambitions or objectives or whatever you may call them. Surely they are rather limited?"

She laughed at this.

"Our main object in life," she said with amusement, "is to be alive. I think your humans may have forgotten this one. Our pleasures, however, if they are to be compared with ornaments and riches, are not so dull as they seem. We have a song about them, called *The Boon of Life*."

"Sing it."

"I will, in a minute. But I must say, before I begin, that it has always seemed a pity to me that one great boon has been left out. The people in the song are supposed to be arguing about the joys of the geese, and nobody mentions travel. I think this is silly. We travel a hundred times further than the humans, and see such interesting things, and have such delightful change and novelty all the time, that I cannot understand how the poet can have forgotten it. Why, my grandmother went to Micklegarth: I had an uncle who had been to Burma: and great-grand-dad used to say he had visited Cuba."

As the king knew that Micklegarth was the Scandinavian name for Constantinople, while he had only heard of Burma from T. natrix, and Cuba had not been invented at all, he was suitably impressed.

"It must be heavenly," he said, "to travel."

He thought of the lovely wings, and of the songs of flight, and of the world pouring, always new and new, beneath their pinions.

"This is the song," she said without further preamble, and she began to sing it gracefully to a wild-goose air:

THE BOON OF LIFE

Ky-yow replied: The boon of life is health.
Paddle-foot, Feather-straight, Supple-neck,
Button-eye:
These have the world's wealth.

Aged Ank answered: Honour is our all.
Path-finder, People-feeder, Plan-provider,
    Sage-commander:
These hear the high call.

Lyó-lyok the lightsome said: Love I had liefer.
Douce-down, Tender-tread, Warm-nest and
    Walk-in-line:
These live forever.

Aahng-ung was for Appetite. Ah, he said,
   Eating!
Gander-gobble, Tear-grass, Stubble-stalk,
   Stuff-crop:
These take some beating.

Wink-wink praised Comrades, the fair free
   fraternity.
Line-astern, Echelon, Arrow-head, Over-cloud:
These learn Eternity.

But I, Lyow, choose Lay-making, of loud lilts
   which linger.
Horn-music, Laughter-song, Epic-heart, Ape-
   the-world:
These Lyow, the singer.

It was a beautiful song in a way, he thought,
given with her tender gravity. He began counting
the boons which she had mentioned on his toes:
but, as he only had three in front and a sort of
knob behind, he had to go round twice. Travel,
health, honour, love, appetite, comradeship,
music, poetry and, as she had stated, being alive
itself.

It did not seem a bad list in its simplicity,
particularly as she might have added something
like Wisdom.

14

BUT THERE WAS a growing excitement among the host. The young geese flirted outrageously, or collected in parties to discuss their pilots. They played games also, like children excited at the prospect of a party. One of these games was to stand in a circle, while the young ganders, one after another, walked into the middle of it with their heads stretched out, pretending to hiss. When they were half-way across the circle they would run the last part, flapping their wings. This was to shew how brave they were, and what excellent admirals they would make, when they grew up. Also the strange habit of shaking their bills sideways, which was usual before flight, began to grow upon them. The elders and sages, who knew the migration routes, became uneasy also. They kept a wise eye on the cloud formations, summing up the wind, and the strength of it, and what airt it was coming from.

The admirals, heavy with responsibility, paced their quarter-decks with ponderous tread.

"Why am I restless?" he asked. "Why do I have this feeling in my blood?"

"Wait and see," she said mysteriously. "Tomorrow, perhaps, or the day after..."

And her eyes assumed the expression of dreams, a look of far away and long ago.

When the morrow came, there was a difference about the salt marsh and the slob. The antlike man, who had walked out so patiently every day to his long nets, with the tides fixed firmly in his head, because to make a mistake in them was certain death, heard a far bugle in the sky. He saw no thousands on the mud-flats, and there were none in the pastures from which he had come. He was a nice little man in his way; for he stood still solemnly, and took off his hat. He did this every spring religiously, when the wild geese left him, and every autumn, when he saw the first returning gaggle.

How far is it across the North Sea? In a steamer it takes us two or three days, so many hours of slobbering through the viscous water. But for the geese, for the sailors of the air, for the angled wedges of heaven tearing clouds to tatters, for those singers of the empyrean with the gale behind them—seventy miles an hour behind another seventy—for those mysterious geographers—three miles up, they say—with cumulus for their floor instead of water: what was it for them? One thing it was, and that was joy.

The king had never seen his friends so gleeful.
The songs they sang, hour after hour, were mad
with it. Some were vulgar, which we shall have to
leave for another time, some were sagas beautiful
beyond comparison, some were lighthearted to a
degree. One silly one which amused him, was as
follows:

> *We wander the sky with many a Cronk*
> *And land in the pasture fields with a Plonk.*
> *Hank-hank, Hink-hink, Honk-honk.*
>
> *Then we bend our necks with a curious kink*
> *Like the bend which the plumber puts under the*
>   *sink.*
> *Honk-honk, Hank-hank, Hink-hink.*
>
> *And we feed away in a sociable rank*
> *Tearing the grass with a sideways yank.*
> *Hink-hink, Honk-honk, Hank-hank.*
>
> *But Hink or Honk we relish the Plonk,*
> *And Honk or Hank we relish the rank,*
> *And Hank or Hink we think it a jink*
>   *To Honk or Hank or Hink!*

A sentimental one was:

> *Wild and free, wild and free,*
> *Bring back my gander to me, to me.*

While, when they were passing over a rocky
island populated by barnacle geese, who all
looked like spinsters in black leather gloves, grey

toques and jet beads, the entire squadron burst out derisively with:

> *Branta bernicla sits a-slumming in the slob,*
> *Branta bernicla sits a-slumming in the slob,*
> *Branta bernicla sits a-slumming in the slob,*
> *   While we go sauntering along.*
> *Glory, glory, here we go, dear.*
> *Glory, glory, here we go, dear.*
> *Glory, glory, here we go, dear.*
> *   To the North Pole sauntering along.*

But it is no good trying to tell about the beauty. It was just that life was beautiful beyond belief, and that is a kind of joy which has to be lived.

Sometimes, when they came down from the cirrus levels to catch a better wind, they would find themselves among the flocks of cumulus: huge towers of modelled vapour, looking as white as Monday's washing and as solid as meringues. Perhaps one of these piled-up blossoms of the sky, these snow-white droppings of a gigantic Pegasus, would lie before them several miles away. They would set their course toward it, seeing it grow bigger silently and imperceptibly, a motionless growth; and then, when they were at it, when they were about to bang their noses with a shock against its seeming solid mass, the sun would dim. Wraiths of mist suddenly moving like serpents of the air would coil about them for a second. Grey damp would be around them, and the sun, a copper penny, would fade away. The wings next

to their own wings would shade into vacancy,
until each bird was a lonely sound in cold
annihilation, a presence after uncertain. And there
they would hang in chartless nothing, seemingly
without speed or left or right or top or bottom,
until as suddenly as ever the copper penny glowed
and the serpents writhed. Then, in a moment of
time, they would be in the jewelled world once
more: a sea under them like turquoise and all the
gorgeous palaces of heaven new created, with the
dew of Eden not yet dry.

One of the peaks of the migration came when
they passed a rock-cliff of the ocean. There were
other peaks, when, for instance, their line of flight
was crossed by an Indian file of Bewick swans
who were off to Abisko, making a noise as they
went like little dogs barking through
handkerchiefs, or when they overtook a horned
owl plodding manfully along, among the warm
feathers of whose back, *so they said*, a tiny wren
was taking her free ride. But the lonely island was
the best of all.

For it was a town of birds. They were all
hatching, all quarrelling, all friendly nevertheless.
On top of the cliff, where the short turf was, there
were myriads of puffins busy with their burrows;
below them, in Razor-bill Street, the birds were
packed so close, and on such narrow ledges, that
they had to stand with their backs to the sea,
holding tight with long toes; in Guillemot Street,
below that, the guillemots held their sharp, toylike
faces upwards, as thrushes do when hatching;
lowest of all, there were the Kittiwake Slums. And
all the birds—who, like humans, only laid one egg

each—were jammed so tight that their heads were interlaced: had so little of this famous living-space of ours that, when a new bird insisted upon landing at a ledge which was already full, one of the other birds had to tumble off. Yet they were all in such good humour, all so cheerful and cockneyfied and teasing one another! They were like an innumerable crowd of fish-wives on the largest grand-stand in the world, breaking out into private disputes, eating out of paper bags, chipping the referee, singing comic songs, admonishing their children and complaining of their husbands. "Move over a bit, auntie," they said, or "Shove along, grandma"; "There's that Flossie gone and sat on the shrimps"; "Put the toffee in your pocket, dearie, and blow yer nose"; "Lawks, if it isn't Uncle Albert with the beer"; "Any room for a little 'un?"; "There goes Aunt Emma, fallen off the ledge"; "Is me hat on straight?"; "Crickey, if this isn't arf a do!"

They kept more or less to their own kind, but they were not mean about it. Here and there, in Guillemot Street, there would be an obstinate kittiwake sitting on a projection and determined to have her rights. Perhaps there were half a million of them, and the noise they made was deafening.

The king could not help wondering how a human town of mixed races would get on, in such conditions.

Then there were the fiords and islands of Norway. It was about one of these islands, by the way, that the great W. H. Hudson related a true goose-story which is liable to make one think.

There was a coastal farmer, he tells us, whose
islands suffered under a nuisance of foxes; so he
set up a fox-trap on one of them. When he visited
the trap the next day, he found that an old wild
goose had been caught in it, obviously a Grand
Admiral, because of his toughness and his heavy
bars. This farmer took the goose home alive,
pinioned it, bound up its leg, and turned it out
with his own ducks and poultry in the farmyard.
Now one of the effects of the fox plague was that
the farmer had to lock his hen-house at night. He
used to go round in the evening to drive them in,
and then he would lock the door. After a time, he
began to notice a curious circumstance, which was
that the hens, instead of having to be collected,
would be found waiting for him in the hut. He
watched the process one evening, and discovered
that the old wild goose had taken upon himself
the responsibility which he had with his own
intelligence observed. Every night at locking-up
time, the sagacious old admiral would round up
his domestic comrades, whose leadership he had
assumed, and would prudently assemble them in
the proper place by his own efforts, as if he had
fully understood the situation. Nor did the free
wild geese, his some-time followers, ever again
settle on the other island—previously a haunt of
theirs—from which their judicious captain had
been spirited away.

Last of all, beyond the islands, there was the
landing at their first day's destination. Oh, the
whiffling of delight and self-congratulation! They
tumbled down out of the sky, sideslipping,

stunting, even doing spinning nose-dives. They were terrifically proud of themselves and of their pilot, agog for the family pleasures which were in store.

They planed for the last part on down-curved wings. At the last moment they scooped the wind with them, flapping them vigorously. Next, bump, they were on the ground. They held their wings above their heads for a moment, then folded them up with a quick and pretty neatness. They had crossed the North Sea.

15

THE SIBERIAN BOGLAND, which they reached a
few days later, was a bowl of sunlight. Its
mountains still retained a lacework of snow,
which, as it melted, brought the little rivers down
in a spate like ale. The lakes glittered under
clouds of mosquitos, and, among the stunted
birch trees round their margins, the amiable
reindeer wandered curiously, snuffling at the
goose-nests, while the geese hissed back at them.

Lyó-lyok settled down at once to build her
nursery, although unmarried, and the king had
time to think.

He was an uncritical man, certainly not a bitter
one. The treachery to which he had been subjected
by his human race had only just begun to weigh
upon him. He had never put it in plain terms to
himself: but the truth was that he had been
betrayed by everybody, even by his own wife and
by his oldest friend. His son was the least of the

traitors. His Table had turned on him, or half of it had, and so had half the country for which he had been working all his life. Now they were asking him to go back into service for the men of treason, and at last he realised, for the first time, that to do so would mean his end. For what hope had he among mankind? They had murdered, almost invariably, every decent person who had spoken to them since the time of Socrates. They had even murdered their God. Anybody who told them the truth was the legitimate object of their treachery, and Merlyn's sentence on himself was one of death.

But here, he realised, among the geese, to whom murder and treason were an obscenity, he was happy and at rest. Here there was good hope for a person with a heart. Sometimes a tired man who has a religious vocation to become a monk will feel an actual yearning for the cloister, for the place where he can expand his soul like a flower and grow towards his idea of good. That is what the old man felt with a sudden longing, except that his cloister was the sun-drenched bog. He wanted to have done with man, to settle down.

To settle down with Lyó-lyok, for instance: it seemed to him that a weary spirit might do worse. He began comparing her wistfully with the women he had known, not always to her disadvantage. She was healthier than they were, nor had she ever had the megrims or the vapours or the hysterics. She was as healthy as himself, as strong, as able on the wing. There was nothing that he could do, which she could not do: so that their community of interests would be exact. She was docile, prudent, faithful, conversable. She was a great deal cleaner than most women, because she spent one half of the day in preening herself and the other half in water, nor were her features disfigured by a single smear of paint. Once she had been married, she would accept no further lovers. She was more beautiful than the average woman, because she possessed a natural shape instead of an artificial one. She was graceful and did not waddle, for all the wild geese do their walking easily, and he had learned to think her plumage handsome. She would be a loving mother.

He found in his old heart a warm feeling for Lyó-lyok, even if there was little passion. He admired her sturdy legs, with the knob at the top, and her neat bill. It had serrations like teeth, and a large tongue which seemed to fill it. He liked her for not being in a hurry.

The nest-making enthralled her, which made him watch it with pleasure. It was not an architectural triumph, but it was what was needed. She had been fussy about the tussock which she meant to choose, and then, after the situation had been finally decided, she had lined the peaty hollow, which was like some soft damp brown and crumbled blotting-paper, or like the tan in a circus, with heather, lichens, moss, and down from her own breast. This was as soft as cob-webs. He had brought her a few bits of grass himself, as a present, but they had generally been of the wrong shape. In plucking them, he had

discovered by accident the wonderful universe of
the bog on which they walked.

For it was a miniature world, the same kind as
the Japanese are said to make in bowls. No
Japanese gardener has ever bred a stunted tree
more like a real one than a stalk of heather is,
with its regular knots along the stalk, like button-
holes. There, at his feet, there were forests of
gnarled trees, with glades and landscapes. There
was the closest moss for grass, and an
undergrowth of lichens. There were fallen tree-
trunks lying picturesquely, and even a strange
kind of flower: a minute grey-green stalk, very dry
and brittle, with a scarlet blob on the end of it,
like sealing-wax. There were microscopic
toadstools, except that their umbrellas turned
upwards, like eggcups. And through the
desiccated sylvan scene there scuttled, for rabbits
and foxes, beetles of a glossy blackness which
looked oily, who adjusted their wings by twirling
their pointed tails. These were the dragons of the
enchantment, rather than the rabbits, and they
were of endless variety: beetles as green as jewels,
spiders as small as pin-heads, lady-birds like red
enamel. In depressions of the peat, which was
resilient to the foot, there were small pools of
brown water populated by sea-dragons: newts and
water-boatmen. Here, in the wetter soil, there was
a riot of mosses, each differing from the other:
some with thin red stalks and green heads, like a
peculiar corn for the Lilliputians. There, where
the heather had been burned by some natural
agency such as the sun shining through a dew

drop—and not by man, who chooses to burn his bogs in the spring time, when they were full of nesting birds—there was a desolation of charred stumps, with tiny snail-shells, bleached white, no bigger than pepper-corns, also putty-coloured lichens like parched sponges, whose stalks were hollow when he broke them up.

And there was the vastness of it, on top of its microscopic size: there was the bog smell and the clean air, which tastes so much wider on bogs: there was the sun, positively pelting it with vigour, who only slept for a couple of hours at night: and, Heaven defend us, there were the mosquitos!

He had often thought that it must be boring for a bird to sit on eggs. He now knew that Lyó-lyok would have a universe to watch before her, a whole world bustling beneath her nose.

He proposed himself one afternoon, not ardently, for he had known the world too long, but gently and hopefully, when they were on the dazzling lake. Its waters, in their frame of brown, reflected the sky to a tone of even deeper blue, as blue as a blackbird's eggs without the spots. He swam towards her with his tail high in the water, his head and neck stretched flat, like a swimming snake. He told her of his sorrows, of his unworthy nature, and of his admiration. He told her how, by joining her, he hoped to escape from Merlyn and the world. Lyó-lyok, as usual, did not seem to be surprised. She too lowered her neck and swam towards him. He was very happy when he saw the douceness of her eyes.

But a dark hand came to fetch him, as you may

have guessed. He found himself swept backwards, not on pinion, not migrating, but dragged down into the filthy funnel of magic. He snatched one floating feather as he vanished, and Lyó-lyok was before his face no more.

16

"Now," CRIED THE MAGICIAN, almost before the traveller had materialised. "Now we can begin to forge ahead with the main idea. We are beginning to see the light at last."

"Give him a chance," said the goat. "He is looking unhappy."

Merlyn swept the suggestion away.

"Unhappy? Nonsense. He is perfectly well. I was saying we could begin to forge ahead..."

"Communism," began the badger, who was short-sighted and wrapped up in the subject.

"No, no. We are finished with the bolsheviks. He is in possession of the data, and we can begin to deal with Might. But he must be allowed to think for himself. King, will you choose any animals you please, and I will explain to you why they do or do not go to war?

"There is no deception," he added, leaning forward as if to press the animals upon his

133

hopeless victim, like sweetmeats, with a
fascinating smile. "You can have any animals you
fancy. Adders, amoebae, antelopes, apes, asses,
axolotls . . ."

"Suppose he has ants and geese," suggested the
badger nervously.

"No, no. Not geese. Geese are too easy. We
must be fair, and let him choose what he pleases.
Suppose we say rooks?"

"Very well," said the badger. "Rooks."

Merlyn leaned back in his chair, put his finger-
tips together, and cleared his throat.

"The first thing," he said, "which we must do
before considering examples, is to define the
subject. What is War? War, I take it, may be
defined as an aggressive use of might between
collections of the same species. It must be between
collections, for otherwise it is mere assault and
battery. An attack of one mad wolf upon a pack
of wolves would not be war. And then again, it
must be between members of the same species.
Birds preying on locusts, cats preying on mice, or
even tunny preying on herrings—that is, fish of
one species preying upon fish of another—none of
these are true examples of war. Thus we see that
there are two essentials: that the combatants
should be of the one family, and that they should
be of a gregarious family. We can therefore begin
by dismissing all animals which are not
gregarious, before we search for examples of
warfare in nature. Having done that, we find
ourselves left with large numbers of animals such
as starlings, minnows, rabbits, bees, and
thousands of others. Upon beginning our search

for warfare among these, however, we find a
dearth of examples. How many animals can you
think of, which take concerted aggressive action
against groups of their own species?"

Merlyn waited two seconds for the old man to
answer, and continued with his lecture.

"Exactly. You were about to mention a few
insects, man, various microbes or blood
corpuscles—if these can be said to be of the same
species—and then you would have been at a loss.
The gross immorality of warfare is, as I
mentioned before, an oddity in nature. We sit
down, therefore, relieved by this fortunate
coincidence of a bundle of data which might have
proved too bulky, and we examine the special
peculiarities of those species which do engage in
hostilities. What do we find? Do we find, as
badger's famous communists would postulate,
that it is the species which owns individual
property that fights? On the contrary, we find that
the warfaring animals are the very ones which
tend to limit or to banish individual possessions.
It is the ants and bees, with their *communal*
stomachs and territories, and the men, with their
national property, who slit each other's throats;
while it is the birds, with their private wives, nests
and hunting grounds, the rabbits with their own
burrows and stomachs, the minnows with their
individual homesteads, and the lyre-birds with
their personal treasure houses and ornamental
pleasure-grounds, who remain at peace. You must
not despise mere nests and hunting grounds as
forms of property: they are as much a form of
property to the animals as a home and business is

to man. And the important thing is that they are private property. The owners of private property in nature are pacific, while those who have invented public property go to war. This, you will observe, is exactly the opposite of the totalist doctrine.

"Of course the owners of private property in nature are sometimes forced to defend their holdings against piracy by other individuals. This rarely results in bloodshed, and men themselves need not fear it, because our king has already persuaded them to adopt the principle of a police force.

"But you want to object that perhaps the link which binds the warfaring animals together is not the link of nationalism: perhaps they go to war for other reasons—because they are all manufacturers, or all owners of domestic animals, or all agriculturalists like some of the ants, or because they all have stores of food. I need not trouble you with a discussion of possibilities, for you must examine them for yourself. Spiders are the greatest of manufacturers, yet do no battle: bees have no domestic animals or agriculture, yet go to war: many ants who are belligerent have no stores of food. By some such mental process as this, as in finding out the Highest Common Factor in mathematics, you will end with the explanation which I have offered: an explanation which is, indeed, self-evident when you come to look at it. War is due to communal property, the very thing which is advocated by nearly all the demagogues who peddle what they call a New Order.

"I have out-run my examples. We must return to the concrete instances, to examine the case. Let us look at a rookery.

"Here is a gregarious animal like the ant, which lives together with its comrades in airy communities. The rookery is conscious of its nationalism to the extent that it will molest other rooks, from distant congeries, if they attempt to build in its own trees. The rook is not only gregarious but also faintly nationalistic. But the important thing is that it does not make any claim to *national property* in its feeding grounds. Any adjacent field that is rich in seed or worms will be frequented not only by the rooks of this community but also by those of all nearby communities, and, indeed, by the jackdaws and pigeons of the neighbourhood, without the outbreak of hostilities. The rooks, in fact, do not claim national property except to the minor extent of their nesting site, and the result is that they are free from the scourge of war. They agree to the obvious natural truth, that access to raw materials must be free to private enterprise.

"Then turn to the geese: one of the oldest races, one of the most cultured, one of the best supplied with language. Admirable musicians and poets, masters of the air for millions of years without ever having dropped a bomb, monogamous, disciplined, intelligent, gregarious, moral, responsible, we find them adamant in their belief that the natural resources of the world cannot be claimed by any particular sect or family of their tribe. If there is a good bed of *Zostera marina* or a good field of stubble, there may be two hundred geese on it today, ten thousand tomorrow. In one skein of geese which is moving from feeding ground to resting place, we may find white-fronts mingled with pink-feet or grey-lags or even with the bernicles. The world is free to all. Yet do not suppose that they are communists. Each individual goose is prepared to assault his neighbour for the possession of a rotten potato, while their wives and nests are strictly private. They have no communal home or stomach, like the ants. And these beautiful creatures, who migrate freely over the whole surface of the globe without making claim to any part of it, have never fought a war.

"It is nationalism, the claims of small communities to parts of the indifferent earth as communal property, which is the curse of man. The petty and drivelling advocates of Irish or Polish nationalism: these are the enemies of man. Yes, and the English, who will fight a major war ostensibly for 'the rights of small nations,' while erecting a monument to a woman who was martyred for the remark that patriotism was not good enough, these people can only be regarded as a collection of benevolent imbeciles conducted by bemused crooks. Nor is it fair to pick on the English or the Irish or the Poles. All of us are in it. It is the general idiocy of *Homo impoliticus*. Aye, and when I speak rudely of the English in this particular, I would like to add at once that I have lived among them during several centuries. Even if they are a collection of imbecile crooks, they are at least bemused and benevolent about it, which I cannot help thinking is preferable to the tyrannous and cynical stupidity of the Huns who fight against them. Make no mistake about that."

"And what," asked the badger politely, "is the practical solution?"

"The simplest and easiest in the world. You must abolish such things as tariff barriers, passports and immigration laws, converting mankind into a federation of individuals. In fact, you must abolish nations, and not only nations but states also; indeed, you must tolerate no unit larger than the family. Perhaps it will be necessary to limit private incomes on a generous scale, for fear that very rich people might become a kind of nation in themselves. That the individuals should be turned into communists or anything else is quite unnecessary, however, and it is against the laws of nature. In the course of a thousand years we should hope to have a common language if we were lucky, but the main thing is that we must make it possible for a man living at Stonehenge to pack up his traps overnight and to seek his fortune without hindrance in Timbuktu . . .

"Man might become migratory," he added as an afterthought, with some surprise.

"But this would spell disaster!" exclaimed the badger. "Japanese labour . . . Trade would be undercut!"

"Fiddlesticks. All men have the same physical structure and need of nourishment. If a coolie can ruin you by living on a bowl of rice in Japan, you had better go to Japan and buy a bowl of rice. Then you can ruin the coolie, who will by then, I suppose, be sporting it in London in your Rolls-Royce."

"But it would be the deathblow of civilisation! It would lower the standard of living..."

"Fudge. It would raise the coolie's standard of living. If he is as good a man as you are in open competition, or a better one, good luck to him. He is the man we want. As for civilisation, look at it."

"It would mean an economic revolution!"

"Would you rather have a series of Armageddons? Nothing of value was ever yet got in this world, my badger, without being paid for."

"Certainly," agreed the badger suddenly, "it seems the thing to do."

"So there you have it. Leave man to his petty tragedy, if he prefers to embrace it, and look about you at two hundred and fifty thousand other animals. They, at any rate, with a few trifling exceptions, have political sense. It is a straight choice between the ant and the goose, and all our king will need to do, when he returns, will be to make their situation obvious."

The badger, who was a faithful opponent to all kinds of exaggeration, objected strongly.

"Surely," he said, "this is a piece of muddled thinking, to say that man may choose between ants and the geese? In the first place man can be neither, and secondly, as we know, the ants are not unhappy as themselves."

Merlyn covered his argument at once.

"I should not have said so. It was a manner of speaking. Actually there are never more than two choices open to a species: either to evolve along its own lines of evolution, or else be liquidated. The ants had to choose between being ants or being extinct, and the geese had to choose between extinction and being geese. It is not that the ants are wrong while the geese are right. Antism is right for ants and goosyness is right for geese. In the same way, man will have to choose between being liquidated and being manly. And a great part of being manly lies in the intelligent solution of these very problems of force, which we have been examining through the eyes of other creatures. That is what the king must try to make them see."

Archimedes coughed and said, "Excuse me, Master, but is your backsight clear enough today, to tell us if he will succeed?"

Merlyn scratched his head and wiped his spectacles.

"He will succeed in the end," he said eventually. "That I am certain of. Otherwise the race must perish like the American wood-pigeons, who, I may add, were considerably more numerous than the human family, yet became extinct in the course of a dozen years at the end of the nineteenth century. But whether it is to be this time or another is still obscure to me. The difficulty of living backwards and thinking forwards is that you become confused about the present. It is also the reason why one prefers to escape into the abstract."

The old gentleman folded his hands upon his stomach, toasted his feet at the fire, and, reflecting upon his own predicament in Time, began to recite from one of his favourite authors.

"I saw," he quoted, "the histories of mortal men of many different races being enacted before my eyes.... kings and queens and emperors and republicans and patricians and plebeians swept in reverse order across my view.... Time rushed backward in tremendous panoramas. Great men died before they won their fame. Kings were deposed before they were crowned. Nero and the Borgias and Cromwell and Asquith and the Jesuits enjoyed eternal infamy and then began to earn it. My motherland ... melted into barbaric Britain; Byzantion melted into Rome; Venice into Henetian Altino; Hellas into innumerable migrations. Blows fell; and then were struck."

In the silence which succeeded this impressive picture, the goat returned to an earlier topic.

"He is looking unhappy," said he, "whatever you may say."

So they looked at the king for the first time since his return and all fell silent.

17

HE WAS WATCHING THEM with the feather in his hand. He held it out unconsciously, his fragment of beauty. He kept them off with it, as if it were a weapon to hold them back.

"I am not going," he said. "You must find another ox to draw for you. Why have you brought me away? Why should I die for man when you speak of him contemptuously yourselves? For it would be death. It is all too true that people are ferocious and stupid. They have given me every sorrow but death. Do you suppose that they will listen to wisdom, that the dullard will understand and throw down his arms? No, he will kill me for it: kill me as the ants would have killed an albino.

"And Merlyn," he cried, "I am afraid to die, because I have never had a chance to live! I never had a life of my own, nor time for beauty, and I had just begun to find it. You shew me beauty,

143

and snatch it from me. You move me like a piece at chess. Have you the right to take my soul and twist it into shapes, to rob a mind of its mind?

"Oh, animals, I have failed you, I know. I have betrayed your trust. But I cannot face the collar again, because you have driven me into it too long. Why should I leave Lyó-lyok? I was never clever, but I was patient, and even patience goes. Nobody can bear it all his life."

They did not dare to answer, could think of nothing to say.

His feeling of guilt and of love frustrated had made him wretched, so that now he had to rage in self-defence.

"Yes, you are clever. You know the long words and how to juggle with them. If the sentence is a pretty one, you laugh and make it. But these are human souls you are cackling about, and it is my soul, the only one I have, which you have put in the index. And Lyó-lyok had a soul. Who made you into gods to meddle with destiny, or set you over hearts to bid them come and go? I will do this filthy work no longer; I will trouble with your filthy plans no further; I will go away into some quiet place with the goose-people, where I can die in peace."

His voice broke down into that of an old and miserable beggar, as he threw himself back in the chair, covering his eyes with his hands.

The urchin was found to be standing in the middle of the floor. With his little, purplish fingers clenched into tight fists, with a truculent nose questing for opposition, breathing heavily, bristling with dead twigs, small, indignant, vulgar and flea-bitten, the hedgehog confronted the committee and faced them down.

"Leave off, wullee?" he demanded. "Stand back, carnt 'ee? Give ter lad fair play."

And he placed his body sturdily between them and his hero, prepared to knock the first man down who interfered.

"Ar," he said sarcastically. "A fine parcel of bougers, us do say. A fine picking o' Bumtious Pilates, for to depose of Man. Gibble-gabble, gibble-gabble. But ding the mun as stirs is finger or us busts un's bloudie neck."

Merlyn protested miserably: "Nobody would have wished him to do anything that he did not want..."

The hedgehog walked up to him, put his twitching nose to within an inch of the magician's spectacles, so that he drew back in alarm, and blew in his face.

"Ar," he said. "Nobody wished nuthink never. Excepting for to remember as 'ee mighter wished suthink for 'isself."

Then he returned to the broken-hearted king, halting at a distance with tact and dignity, because of his fleas.

"Nay, Mëaster," he said. "Tha hast been within too long. Let thee come art along of a nugly hurchin, that tha mayest sniff God's air to thy nostrils, an lay thy head to the boozum o' the earth.

"Tëak no thought fer them bougers," he continued. "Lave 'un fer to argyfy theirselves inter the hy-stericks, that 'ull plaze 'un. Let thee smell a

peck of air wi' ter humble mun, an have thy pleasure of the sky."

Arthur held out his hand for the urchin's, who gave it reluctantly, after wiping it on the prickles of his back.

"He'm verminous," he explained regretfully, "but he'm honest."

They went together to the door, where the hedgehog, turning round, surveyed the field.

"Orryvoyer," he observed good-humouredly, regarding the committee with ineffable contempt. "Mind yer doant destroy ter universt afore as we comes back. No creating of another, mind."

And he bowed sarcastically to the stricken Merlyn.

"God ter Father."

To the wretched Archimedes, who elongated himself, closed his eyes, and looked the other way.

"God ter Son."

To the imploring badger.

"And God ter Holy Post."

18

THERE IS NOTHING so wonderful as to be out on a spring night in the country; but really in the latest part of night, and, best of all, if you can be alone. Then, when you can hear the wild world scamper, and the cows chewing just before you tumble over them, and the leaves living secretly, and the nibblings and grass pluckings and the blood's tide in your own veins: when you can see the loom of the trees and hills in deeper darkness and the stars twirling in their oiled grooves for yourself: when there is one light in one cottage far away, marking a sickness or an early riser upon a mysterious errand: when the horse hoofs with squeaking cart behind plod to an unknown market, dragging their bundled man, in sacks, asleep: when the dogs' chains rattle at the farms, and the vixen yelps once, and the owls have fallen silent: then is a grand time to be alive and vastly conscious, when all else human is unconscious, homebound, bed-sprawled, at the mercy of the midnight mind.

The wind had dropped to rest. The powdery stars expanded and contracted in the serene, making a sight which would have jingled, if it had been a sound. The great tor which they were climbing rose against the sky, a mire of majesty, like a horizon which aspired.

The little hedgehog, toiling from tussock to tussock, fell into the marshy puddles with grunts, panted as he struggled with the miniature cliffs. The weary king gave him a hand at the worst places, hoisting him into a better foothold or giving him a shove behind, noticing how pathetic and defenceless his bare legs looked from the back.

"Thank 'ee," he said. "Much obliged, us 'm sure."

When they had reached the top, he sat down puffing, and the old man sat beside him to admire the view.

It was England that came out slowly, as the late moon rose: his royal realm of Gramarye. Stretched at his feet, she spread herself away into the remotest north, leaning towards the imagined Hebrides. She was his homely land. The moon made her trees more important for their shadows than for themselves, picked out the silent rivers in quicksilver, smoothed the toy pasture fields, laid a soft haze on everything. But he felt that he would have known the country, even without the light. He knew that there must be the Severn, there the Downs and there the Peak: all invisible to him, but inherent in his home. In this field a white horse must be grazing, in that some washing must be hanging on a hedge. It had a necessity to be itself.

He suddenly felt the intense sad loveliness of being as being, apart from right or wrong: that, indeed, the mere fact of being was the ultimate right. He began to love the land under him with a fierce longing, not because it was good or bad, but because it was: because of the shadows of the corn stooks on a golden evening; because the sheep's tails would rattle when they ran, and the lambs, sucking, would revolve their tails in little eddies; because the clouds in daylight would surge it into light and shade; because the squadrons of green and golden plover, worming in pasture fields, would advance in short, unanimous charges, head to wind; because the spinsterish herons, who keep their hair up with fish bones according to David Garnett, would fall down in a faint if a boy could stalk them and shout before he was seen; because the smoke from homesteads was a blue beard straying into heaven; because the stars were righter in puddles than in the sky; because there were puddles, and leaky gutters, and dung hills with poppies on them; because the salmon in the rivers suddenly leaped and fell; because the chestnut buds, in the balmy wind of spring, would jump out of their twigs like jacks-in-boxes, or like little spectres holding up green hands to scare him; because the jackdaws, building, would hang in the air with branches in their mouths, more beautiful than any ark-returning dove; because, in the moonlight there below, God's greatest blessing to the world was stretched, the silver gift of sleep.

He found that he loved it—more than

Guenever, more than Lancelot, more than Lyó-
lyok. It was his mother and his daughter. He
knew the speech of its people, would have felt it
change beneath him, if he could have shot across
it like the goose which once he was, from
Zumerzet to Och-aye. He could tell how the
common people would feel about things, about all
sorts of things, before he asked them. He was
their king.

And they were his people, his own
responsibility of *stultus* or *ferox,* a responsibility
like that old goose-admiral's upon the farm. They
were not ferocious now, because they were asleep.

England was at the old man's feet, like a
sleeping man-child. When it was awake it would
stump about, grabbing things and breaking them,
killing butterflies, pulling the cat's tail, nourishing
its ego with amoral and relentless mastery. But in
sleep its masculine force was abdicated. The man-
child sprawled undefended now, vulnerable, a
baby trusting the world to let it sleep in peace.

All the beauty of his humans came upon him,
instead of their horribleness. He saw the vast
army of martyrs who were his witnesses: young
men who had gone out even in the first joy of
marriage, to be killed on dirty battle-fields like
Bedegraine for other men's beliefs: but who had
gone out voluntarily: but who had gone because
they thought it was right: but who had gone
although they hated it. They had been ignorant
young men perhaps, and the things which they
had died for had been useless. But their ignorance
had been innocent. They had done something
horribly difficult in their ignorant innocence,

which was not for themselves.

He saw suddenly all the people who had accepted sacrifice: learned men who had starved for truth, poets who had refused to compound in order to achieve success, parents who had swallowed their own love in order to let their children live, doctors and holy men who had died to help, millions of crusaders, generally stupid, who had been butchered for their stupidity—but who had meant well.

That was it, to mean well! He caught a glimpse of that extraordinary faculty in man, that strange, altruistic, rare and obstinate decency which will make writers or scientists maintain their truths at the risk of death. *Eppur si muove,* Galileo was to say; it moves all the same. They were to be in a position to burn him if he would go on with it, with his preposterous nonsense about the earth moving round the sun, but he was to continue with the sublime assertion because there was something which he valued more than himself. The Truth. To recognise and to acknowledge What Is. That was the thing which man could do, which his English could do, his beloved, his sleeping, his now defenceless English. They might be stupid, ferocious, unpolitical, almost hopeless. But here and there, oh so seldom, oh so rare, oh so glorious, there were those all the same who would face the rack, the executioner, and even utter extinction, in the cause of something greater than themselves. Truth, that strange thing, the jest of Pilate's. Many stupid young men had thought they were dying for it, and many would continue to die for it, perhaps for a thousand years. They did not have to be right about their truth, as Galileo was to be. It was enough that they, the few and martyred, should establish a greatness, a thing above the sum of all they ignorantly had.

But then again there came the wave of sorrow over him, the thought of the man-child when he woke: the thought of that cruel and brutish majority, to whom the martyrs were such rare exceptions. It moves, for all that. How few and pitifully few the ones who would be ready to maintain it!

He could have wept for the pity of the world, its horribleness which still was pitiful.

The hedgehog remarked: "Pretty place, annit?"

"Aye, mun. But there is nowt that I can do for 'un."

"Tha hast done champion."

A cottage woke in the valley. Its eye of light winked out, and he could feel the man who had made it: a poacher probably, somebody as slow and clumsy and patient as the badger, pulling on his heavy boots.

The hedgehog asked: "Shire?"

"Sire, mun: and 'tis Majesty, not Maggy's tea."

"Majesty?"

"Aye, mun."

"Dost tha mind as how us used to sing to 'un?"

"I minds 'un well. 'Twas *Rustic Bridge,* and *Genevieve* and ... and ..."

"*Home Sweet Home.*"

The king quite suddenly bowed his head.

"Shall us sing 'un for 'ee agëan, Majesty mun?"

He could only nod.

The hedgehog stood in the moonlight,

assuming the proper attitude for song. He planted his feet squarely, folded his hands on his stomach, fixed his eye upon a distant object. Then, in his clear country tenor, he sang for the King of England about Home Sweet Home.

The silly, simple music died away—but not silly in the moonlight, not on a mountain of your realm. The hedgehog shuffled, coughed, was wistful for something more. But the king was speechless.

"Majesty," he mentioned shyly, "us gotter fresh 'un."

There was no reply.

"When us knowed as you was acoming, us larned a fresh 'un. 'Twas for thy welcome, like. Us larned it off of that there Mëarn."

"Sing it," gasped the old man. He had stretched his bones upon the heather, because it was all too much.

And there, upon the height of England, in a good pronunciation because he had learned it carefully from Merlyn, to Parry's music from the future, with his sword of twigs in one grey hand and a chariot of mouldy leaves, the hedgehog stood to build Jerusalem: and meant it.

> *Give me my bow of burning gold.*
> *Bring me my arrows of desire.*
> *Bring me my spear. Oh, clouds unfold.*
> *Bring me my chariot of fire.*
> *I will not cease from mental strife*
> *Nor shall my sword sleep in my hand*
> *Till I have built Jerusalem*
> *On England's green and pleasant land.*

19

THE PALE FACES OF THE COMMITTEE, hunched
round the fire, turned towards the door in a single
movement, and six pairs of guilty eyes were
fastened on the king. But it was England who
came in.

There was no need to say anything, no need to
explain: they could see it in his face.

Then they were rising up, and coming towards
him, and standing round him humbly. Merlyn, to
his surprise, was an old man with hands which
shook like leaves. He was blowing his nose very
much indeed on his own skull-cap, from which
there was falling a perfect shower of mice and
frogs. The badger was weeping bitterly, and
absent-mindedly swatting each tear as it appeared
on the end of his nose. Archimedes had turned his
head completely back to front, to hide his shame.
Cavall's expression was of torment. T. natrix had
laid his head on the royal foot, with one clear tear

in each nostril. And Balin's nictating membrane was going with the speed of the Morse code.

"God save the king," they said.

"You may be seated."

So they sat down deferentially, after he had taken the first seat: a Privy Council.

"We will be returning soon," he said, "to our bright realm. Before we go, there are questions we must ask. In the first place, it has been said that there will be a man like John Ball; who is to be a bad naturalist because he claims that men should live like ants. What is the objection to his claim?"

Merlyn stood up and took off his hat.

"It is a matter of natural morality, Sir. The committee suggests that it is moral for a species to specialise in its own speciality. An elephant must attend to its trunk, a giraffe or camelopard to its neck. It would be immoral for an elephant to fly, because it has no wings. The speciality of man, as much developed in him as the neck is in the camelopard, is his neopallium. This is the part of the brain which, instead of being devoted to instinct, is concerned with memory, deduction and the forms of thought which result in recognition by the individual of his personality. Man's top-knot makes him conscious of himself as a separate being, which does not often happen in animals and savages, so that any form of pronounced collectivism in politics is contrary to the specialisation of man.

"This, by the way," continued the old gentleman slowly, drawing a film over his eyes as if he were a weary, second-sighted vulture, "is why

I have, during a lifetime extending backwards over several tiresome centuries, waged my little war against might under all its forms, and it is why I have rightly or wrongly seduced others into waging it. It is why I once persuaded you, Sir, to regard the Games-Maniac with contempt: to oppose your wisdom against the baron of Fort Mayne: to believe in justice rather than in power: and to investigate with mental integrity, as we have tried to do this long-drawn evening, the causes of the battle we are waging: for war is force unbridled, at a gallop. I have not engaged in this crusade because the fact of force can be considered wrong, in an abstract sense. For the boa-constrictor, who is practically one enormous muscle, it would be literally true to say that Might is Right: for the ant, whose brain is not constituted like the human brain, it is literally true that the State is more important than the Individual. But for man, whose speciality lies in the personality-recognising creases of his neopallium—as much developed in him as the muscles are in the boa-constrictor—it is equally true to say that mental truth, not force, is right; and that the Indivdual is more important than the State. He is so much more important that he should abolish it. We must leave the boa-constrictors to admire themselves for being muscular athletes: Games-Mania, Fort Mayne and so forth are right for them. Perhaps the reticulations of the python are really some form of 1st XI jersey. We must leave the ants to assert the glory of the state: totalitarianism is their line of country, no doubt. But for man, and not on an abstract definition of right and wrong, but on nature's concrete definition that a species must specialise in its own speciality, the committee suggests that might was never right: that the state never excelled the individual: and that the future lies with the personal soul."

"Perhaps you ought to speak about the brain."

"Sir, there are a great many things going on in this old brain-box; but for the purposes of our investigation we confine ourselves to two compartments, the neopallium and the corpus striatum. In the latter, to put it simply, my instinctive and mechanical actions are determined: in the former I keep that reason in honour of which our race has curiously been nicknamed *sapiens*. Perhaps I can explain it with one of those dangerous and often misleading similes. The corpus striatum is like a single mirror, which reflects instinctive actions outwards, in return for the stimuli which come in. In the neopallium, however, there are two mirrors. *They can see each other, and for that reason they know that they exist.* Man, know thyself, said somebody or other: or, as another philosopher had put it, the proper study of mankind is man. This is because he has specialised in the neopallium. In brainy animals other than man, the emphasis is not on the doublemirrored room, but on the single one. Few animals, except man, are conscious of their own personality. Even in primitive races of the human family there still exists a confusion between the individual and his surroundings—for the savage Indian, as you may know, distinguishes so little between himself and the outside world that he himself will spit, if he wants the clouds to rain. The ant's nervous system may be said to be a single mirror like the savage's, and that is why it suits the ant to be a communist, to lose himself in a crowd. But it is because civilised man's brain is a double-mirror that he will always have to specialise in individuality, in recognition of himself, or whatever you may like to call it: it is because of the two mirrors reflecting each other that he can never wholly succeed as an unselfish member of the proletariat. He must have a self and all that goes with a self so highly developed—including selfishness and property. Pray forgive my simile, if I have seemed to use it unfairly."

"Has the goose a neopallium?"

Merlyn stood up again.

"Yes, a fairly good one for a bird. The ants have a different form of nervous system, on the lines of the corpora striata."

"The second question deals with War. It has been suggested that we ought to abolish it, in one way or another, but nobody has given it the chance to speak for itself. Perhaps there is something to be said in favour of war. We would like to be told."

Merlyn put his hat on the floor and whispered to the badger, who, after scuttling off to his pile of agenda, returned, to the wonder of all, with the proper piece of paper.

"Sir, this question has been before the attention of the committee, who have ventured to draw up a list of Pros and Cons, which we are ready to recite."

Merlyn cleared his throat, and announced in a loud voice: "PRO."

"In favour of war," explained the badger.

"Number One," said Merlyn. "War is one of the mainsprings of romance. Without war, there would be no Rolands, Maccabees, Lawrences or Hodsons of Hodson's Horse. There would be no Victoria Crosses. It is a stimulant to so-called virtues, such as courage and co-operation. In fact, war has moments of glory. It should also be noted that, without war, we should lose at least one half of our literature. Shakespeare is packed with it.

"Number Two. War is a way of keeping down the population, though it is a hideous and inefficient one. The same Shakespeare, who seems on the subject of war to have been in agreement with the Germans and with their raving apologist Nietzsche, says, in a scene which he is supposed to have written for Beaumont & Fletcher, that it heals with blood the earth when it is sick and cures the world of the pleurisy of people. Perhaps I may mention in parentheses, without irreverence, that the Bard seems to have been curiously insensitive on the subject of warfare. *King Henry V* is the most revolting play I know, as Henry himself is the most revolting character.

"Number Three. War does provide a vent for the pent-up ferocity of man, and, while man remains a savage, something of the sort seems to be needed. The committee finds from an examination of history that human cruelty will vent itself in one way, if it is denied another. During the eighteenth and nineteenth centuries, when war was a limited exercise confined to professional armies recruited from the criminal classes, the general mass of the population resorted to public executions, dental operations without anaesthetics, brutal sports and flogging their children. In the twentieth century, when war was extended to embrace the masses, hanging, hacking, cock-fighting and spanking went out of fashion.

"Number Four. The committee is at present occupied about a complicated investigation into the physical or psychological necessity. We do not feel that a report can be made at this stage with profit, but we think we have observed that war does answer a real need in man, perhaps connected with the ferocity mentioned in Article Three, but perhaps not. It has come to our notice that man becomes restless or dejected after a generation of Peace. The immortal if not omniscient Swan of Avon remarks that Peace seems to breed a disease, which, coming to a head in a sort of ulcer, bursts out into war. 'War,' he says, 'is the imposthume of much wealth and peace, which only breaks, shewing no outward cause why the man dies.' Under this interpretation, it is the peace which is regarded as a slow disease, while the bursting of the imposthume, the war, must be assumed to be beneficial rather than the reverse. The committee has suggested two ways in which Wealth and Peace might destroy the race, if war were prevented: by emasculating it, or by rendering it comatose through glandular troubles. On the subject of emasculation, it should be noted that wars double the birth-rate. The reason why women tolerate war is because it promotes virility in men.

"Number Five. Finally, there is the suggestion which would probably be made by every other animal on the face of this earth, except man, namely that war is an inestimable boon to creation as a whole, because it does offer some faint hope of exterminating the human race.

"CON," announced the magician: but the king prevented him.

"We know the objections," he said. "The idea that it is useful might be considered a little more. If there is some necessity for Might, why is the committee ready to stop it?"

"Sir, the committee is attempting to trace the physiological basis, possibly of a pituitary or adrenal origin. Possibly the human system requires periodical doses of adrenalin, in order to remain healthy. (The Japanese, as an instance of glandular activity, are said to eat large quantities of fish, which, by charging their bodies with iodine, expands their thyroids and makes them touchy.) Until this matter has been properly investigated the subject remains vague, but the committee desires to point out that the physiological need could be supplied by other means. War, it has already been observed, is an inefficient way of keeping down the population: it may also be an inefficient way of stimulating the adrenal glands through fear."

"What other ways?"

"Under the Roman Empire, the experiment of offering bloody spectacles in the circus was attempted as a substitute. They provided the

Purgation which Aristotle talks about, and some such alternative might be found efficient. Science, however, would suggest more radical cures. Either the glandular deficiency might be supplied by periodical injections of the whole population with adrenalin—or with whatever the deficiency may prove to be—or else some form of surgery might be found effective. Perhaps the root of war is removable, like the appendix."

"We were told that war is caused by National Property: now we are told that it is due to a gland."

"Sir, the two things may be related, though they may not be consequent upon one another. For instance, if wars were solely due to national property, we should expect them to continue without intermission so long as national property continued: that is, all the time. We find, however, that they are interrupted by frequent lulls, called Peace. It seems as if the human race becomes more and more comatose during these periods of truce, until, when what you may call the saturation-point of adrenalin deficiency has been reached, it seizes upon the first handy excuse for a good shot of fear-stimulant. The handy excuse is national property. Even if the wars are dolled up as religious ones, such as crusades against Saladin or the Albigensians or Montezuma, the basis remains the same. Nobody would have troubled to extend the benefits of Christianity to Montezuma, if his sandals had not been made of gold, and nobody would have thought the gold itself a sufficient temptation, if they had not been needing a dose of adrenalin."

"You suggest an alternative like the circus, pending the investigation of your gland. Have you considered it?"

Archimedes giggled unexpectedly.

"Merlyn wants to have an international fair, Sir. He wants to have a lot of flip-flaps and giant wheels and scenic railways in a reservation, and they are all to be slightly dangerous, so as to kill perhaps one man in a hundred. Entrance is to be voluntary, for he says that the one unutterably wicked thing about a war is conscription. He says that people will go to the fair of their own free-will, through boredom or through adrenalin deficiency or whatever it is, and that they are likely to feel the need for it during their twenty-fifth, thirtieth, and forty-fifth years. It is to be made fashionable and glorious to go. Every visitor will get a commemorative medal, while those who go fifty times will get what he calls the D.S.O. or the V.C. for a hundred visits."

The magician looked ashamed and cracked his fingers.

"The suggestion," he said humbly, "was more to provide thought, than to be thought of."

"Certainly it does not seem a practical suggestion for the present year of grace. Are there no panaceas for war, which could be used in the meantime?"

"The committee has suggested an antidote which might have a temporary effect, like soda for an acid stomach. It would be of no use as a cure for the malady, though it might alleviate it. It might save a few million lives in a century."

"What is this antidote?"

"Sir, you will have noticed that the people who are responsible for the declaration and the higher conduct of wars do not tend to be the people who endure their extremes. At the battle of Bedegraine Your Majesty dealt with something of the same sort. The kings and the generals and the leaders of battles have a peculiar aptitude for not being killed in them. The committee has suggested that, after every war, all the officials on the losing side who held a higher rank than colonel ought to be executed out of hand, irrespective of their warguilt. No doubt there would be a certain amount of injustice in this measure, but the consciousness that death was the certain result of losing a war would have a deterrent effect on those who help to promote and to regulate such engagements, and it might, by preventing a few wars, save millions of lives among the lower classes. Even a Führer like Mordred might think twice about heading hostilities, if he knew that his own execution would be the result of being unlucky in them."

"It seems reasonable."

"It is less reasonable than it seems, partly because the responsibility for warfare does not lie wholly with the leaders. After all, a leader has to be chosen or accepted by those whom he leads. The hydra-headed multitudes are not so innocent as they like to pretend. They have given a mandate to their generals, and they must abide by the moral responsibility."

"Still, it would have the effect of making the leaders reluctant to be pushed into warfare by their followers, and even that would help."

"It would help. The difficulty would lie in

persuading the leading classes to agree to such a convention in the first place. Also, I am afraid that you will find there is always a type of maniac, anxious for notoriety at any price, or even for martyrdom, who would accept the pomp of leadership with even greater alacrity because it was enhanced by melodramatic penalties. The kings of Irish mythology were compelled by their station to march in the forefront of the battle, which occasioned a frightful mortality among them, yet there never seems to have been a lack of kings or battles in the history of the Green Isle."

"What about this new-fangled Law," asked the goat suddenly, "which our king has been inventing? If individuals can be deterred from murder by fear of a death penalty, why cannot there be an international law, under which nations can be deterred from war by similar means? An aggressive nation might be kept at peace by the knowledge that, if it began a war, some international police force would sentence it to dispersal, by mass transportation to other countries for instance."

"There are two objections to that. First, you would be trying to cure the disease, not to prevent it. Second, we know from experience that the existence of a death penalty does not in fact abolish murder. It might, however, prove to be a temporary step in the right direction."

The old man folded his hands in his sleeves, like a Chinaman, and looked round the council table, doggedly, waiting for further questions. His eyes had begun to discharge their watch.

"He has been writing a book called the *Libellus*

Merlini, the *Prophecies of Merlyn,*" continued Archimedes wickedly, when he saw that this subject had been concluded, "which he had intended to read aloud to Your Majesty, as soon as you arrived."

"We will hear a reading."

Merlyn wrung his hands.

"Sir," he said. "It is mere fortune-telling, only gypsy tricks. It had to be written because there was a good deal of fuss about it in the twelfth century, after which we are to lose sight of it until the twentieth. But, oh Sir, it is merely a parlour game—not worth Your Majesty's attention at present."

"Read me some part of it, none the less."

So the humiliated scientist, all of whose quips and quiddities had been knocked out of him in the last hour, fetched the burnt manuscript from the fender and handed round a collection of such slips as were still legible, as if it had been a parlour game in earnest. The animals read them out in turn, like mottos from crackers, and this is what they said:

"God will provide, the Dodo will remark."

"The Bear will cure his headache by cutting off his head—but it will leave him with a sore behind."

"The Lion will lie down with the Eagle, saying, At last all the animals are united! But the Devil will see the joke."

"The Stars which taught the Sun to rise must agree with him at noon—or vanish."

"A child standing in Broadway will cry, Look mother, there is a man!"

"How long it takes to build Jerusalem, the spider will say, pausing exhausted at his web on the ground floor of the Empire State Building."

"Living-space leads to space for the coffin, observed the Beetle."

"Force makes force."

"Wars of community, county, country, creed, continent, colour. After that the hand of God, if not before."

"Imitation (μίμησι s) before action will save mankind."

"The Elk died because it grew its horns too big."

"No collision with the moon was required to exterminate the Mammoth."

"The destiny of all species is extinction as such, fortunately for them."

There was a pause after the last motto, while the listeners thought them over.

"What is the meaning of the one with the Greek word?"

"Sir, a part of its meaning, but only a small part, is that the one hope for our human race must lie in education without coercion. Confucius has it that:

In order to propagate virtue to the world, one must first rule one's country.
In order to rule one's country, one must first rule one's family.
In order to rule one's family, one must first regulate one's body by moral training.

*In order to regulate one's body, one must first
    regulate one's mind.*

*In order to regulate the mind, one must first be
    sincere in one's intentions.*

*In order to be sincere in one's intentions, one
    must first increase one's knowledge."*

"I see."

"Have the rest any relevant meaning?" added
the king.

"None whatever."

"One further question before we rise. You have
said that politics are out of order, but they seem
so closely tied to the question of warfare that they
must be faced to some extent. At an earlier stage
you claimed to be a capitalist. Are you sure of
these views?"

"If I said so, Your Majesty, I did not mean it.
Badger was talking at me like a communist of the
nineteen-twenties, which made me talk like a
capitalist in self-defence. I am an anarchist, like
any other sensible person. In point of fact the race
will find that capitalists and communists modify
themselves so much during the ages that they end
by being indistinguishable as democrats: and so
will the fascists modify themselves, for that
matter. But whatever may be the contortions
adopted by these three brands of collectivism, and
however many the centuries during which they
butcher each other out of childish ill-temper, the
fact remains that *all* forms of collectivism are
mistaken, according to the human skull. The
destiny of man is an individualistic destiny, and it
is in that sense that I may have implied a qualified

approval of capitalism, if I did imply it. The despised Victorian capitalist, who did at least allow a good deal of play to the individual, was probably more truly *futuristic* in his politics than all the New Orders shrieked for in the twentieth century. He was of the future, because individualism lies in the future of the human brain. He was not so old-fashioned as the fascists and communists. But of course he was considerably old-fashioned for all that, and that is why I prefer myself to be an anarchist: that is, to be a little up-to-date. The geese are anarchists, you remember. They realise that the moral sense must come from inside, not from outside."

"I thought," said the badger plaintively, "that communism was supposed to be a step towards anarchy. I thought that when communism had been properly achieved the state would wither away."

"People have told me so, but I doubt it. I cannot see how you may emancipate an individual by first creating an omnipotent state. There are no states in nature, except among monstrosities like the ants. It seems to me that people who go creating states, as Mordred is trying to do with his Thrashers, must tend to become involved in them, and so unable to escape. But perhaps what you say is true. I hope it is. In any case let us leave these dubious questions of politics to the dingy tyrants who look after them. Ten thousand years from now it may be time for the educated to concern themselves with such things, but meanwhile they must wait for the race to grow up. We for our part have offered a solution this

evening to the special problem of force as an
arbiter: the obvious platitude that war is due to
national property, with the rider that it is
stimulated by certain glands. Let us leave it at that
for the present, in God's name."

The old magician swept his notes away with a
trembling hand. He had been deeply wounded by
the hedgehog's earlier criticisms, because, in the
secrecy of his heart, he loved his student dearly.
He knew now, since the royal hero had returned
victorious in his choice, that his own wisdom was
not the end. He knew that he had finished his
tutorship. Once he had told the king that he
would never be the Wart again: but it had been an
encouraging thing to say: he had not meant it.
Now he did mean it, now knew that he himself
had yielded place, had stepped down from the
authority to lead or to direct. The abdication had
cost him his gaiety. He would not be able to rant
any more, or to twinkle and mystify with the
flashing folds of his magic cloak. The
condescension of learning was pricked in him. He
was feeling ancient and ashamed.

The old king, whose childhood had vanished
also, toyed with a slip left on the table. He was at
his trick of watching his hands, when in
abstraction. He folded the paper this way, that
way, carefully, and unfolded it. It was one of
Merlyn's notes for the card-index, which badger
had muddled with the *Prophecies:* a quotation
from a historian called Friar Clynn, who had died
in 1348. This friar, employed as the annalist of his
abbey to keep the historical records, had seen the
Black Death coming to fetch him—possibly to

fetch the whole world, for it had killed a third of the population of Europe already. Carefully leaving some pieces of blank parchment with the book in which he was to write no longer, he had concluded with the following message, which had once awakened Merlyn's strange respect. "Seeing these many ills," he had written in Latin, "and as it were the whole world thrust into malignancy, waiting among the dead for death to come to me, I have put into writing what I have truthfully heard and examined. And, lest the writing should perish with the writer or the work fail with the workman, I am now leaving some paper for the continuation of it—in case by any chance a man may remain alive in the future, or any person of the race of Adam may escape this pestilence, to carry on the labour once begun by me."

The king folded it neatly, measured it on the table. They watched him, knowing he was about to rise and ready to follow his example.

"Very good," he said. "We understand the puzzle."

He tapped the table with the paper, then got to his feet.

"We must return before the morning."

The animals were rising too. They were conducting him to the door, crowding round him to kiss his hand and bid farewell. His now retired tutor, who must conduct him home, was holding the door for him to pass. Whether he was a dream or not, he had begun to flicker, as had they all. They were saying "Good success to Your Majesty, a speedy and successful issue."

He smiled gravely, saying: "We hope it will be speedy."

But he was referring to his death, as one of them knew.

"It is only for this time, Majesty," said T. natrix. "You remember the story of St. George, and *Homo sapiens* is like that still. You will fail because it is the nature of man to slay, in ignorance if not in wrath. But failure builds success and nature changes. A good man's example always does instruct the ignorant and lessens their rage, little by little through the ages, until the spirit of the waters is content: and so, strong courage to Your Majesty, and a tranquil heart."

He inclined his head to the one who knew, and turned to go.

At the last moment a hand was tugging at his sleeve, reminding him of the friend he had forgotten. He lifted the hedgehog with both hands under its armpits, and held it at arm's length, face to face.

"Ah, tiggy," he said. "Us have thee to thank for royalty. Farewell, tiggy, and a merry life to thee and thy sweet songs."

But the hedgehog paddled its feet as if it were bicycling, because it wanted to be put down. It tugged the sleeve again, when it was safe upon the floor, and the old man lowered his ear to hear the whisper.

"Nay, nay," it mentioned hoarsely, clutching his hand, looking earnestly in his face. "Say not Farewell."

It tugged again, dropping its voice to the brink of silence.

"Orryvoyer," whispered the urchin.
"Orryvoyer."

20

WELL, WE HAVE REACHED IT AT LAST, the end of our winding story.

Arthur of England went back to the world, to do his duty as well as he could. He called a truce with Mordred, having made up his mind that he must offer half his kingdom for the sake of peace. To tell the truth, he was prepared to yield it all if necessary. As a possession it had long ceased to be of value to him, and he had come to know for sure that peace was more important than a kingdom. But he felt it was his duty to retain a half if he could, and it was for this reason: that if he had even half a world to work on, he might be able still to introduce, in it, the germs of that good sense which he had learned from geese and animals.

The truce was made, the armies drawn up in their battles, face to face. Each had a standard made from a ship's mast set on wheels, at the top of which a small box held the consecrated Host, while, from the masts, there flew the banners of the Dragon and the Thistle. The knights of Mordred's party were dressed in sable armour, their plumes were sable also, and, on their arms, the scarlet whip of Mordred's badge glared with the sinister tint of blood. Perhaps they looked more terrible than they felt. It was explained to the waiting ranks that none of them must make a hostile demonstration, but all must keep their swords in sheath. Only, for fear of treachery, it was told that they might charge to rescue, if any sword was seen unharnessed at the parley.

Arthur went forward to the space between the armies with his staff, and Mordred, with his own staff in their black accoutrements, came out to meet him. They encountered, and the old king saw his son's face once again. It was taut and haggard.

He too, poor man, had strayed beyond Sorrow and Solitude to the country of Kennaquhair; but he had gone without a guide and lost his way.

The treaty was agreed on, to the surprise of all, more easily than had been hoped. The king was left with half his realm. For a moment joy and peace were in the balance.

But, at that knife-edge of a moment, the old Adam reared itself in a different form. The feudal war, baronial oppression, individual might, even ideological rebellion: he had settled them all in one way or another, only to be beaten on the last lap now, by the epeisodic fact that man was a slayer by instinct.

A grass-snake moved in the meadow near their feet, close to an officer of Mordred's staff. This officer stepped back instinctively and swung his hand across his body, his armlet with the whip

shewing for a second's flash. The bright sword
flamed into being, to destroy the so-called viper.
The waiting armies, taking it for treachery, raised
their shout of rage. The lances on both sides
bowed to rest. And, as King Arthur ran towards
his own array, an old man with white hair trying
to stem the endless tide, holding out the knuckled
hands in a gesture of pressing them back,
struggling to the last against the flood of Might
which had burst out all his life at a new place
whenever he had dammed it, so the tumult rose,
the war-yell sounded, and the meeting waters
closed above his head.

Lancelot arrived too late. He had made his best
speed, but it had been in vain. All he could do was
to pacify the country and give burial to the dead.
Then, when a semblance of order had been
restored, he hurried to Guenever. She was
supposed to be in the Tower of London still, for
Mordred's siege had failed.

But Guenever had gone.

In those days the rules of convents were not so
strict as they are now. Often they were more like
hostelries for their well-born patrons. Guenever
had taken the veil at Amesbury.

She felt that they had suffered enough, and had
caused enough suffering to others. She refused to
see her ancient lover or to talk it over. She said,
which was patently untrue, that she wished to
make her peace with God.

Guenever never cared for God. She was a good
theologian, but that was all. The truth was that
she was old and wise: she knew that Lancelot did

care for God more passionately, that it was essential he should turn in that direction. So, for his sake, to make it easier for him, the great queen now renounced what she had fought for all her life, now set the example, and stood by her choice. She had stepped out of the picture.

Lancelot guessed a good deal of this, and, when she refused to see him, he climbed the convent wall with Gallic, ageing gallantry. He waylaid her to expostulate, but she was adamant and brave. Something about Mordred seems to have broken her lust for life. They parted, never to meet on earth.

Guenever became a wordly abbess. She ruled her convent efficiently, royally, with a sort of grand contempt. The little pupils of the school were brought up in the great tradition of nobility. They saw her walking in the grounds, upright, rigid, her fingers flashing with hard rings, her linen clean and fine and scented against the rules of her order. The novices worshipped her unanimously, with schoolgirl passions, and whispered about her past. She became a Grand Old Lady. When she died at last, her Lancelot came for the body, with his snow-white hair and wrinkled cheeks, to carry it to her husband's grave. There, in the reputed grave, she was buried: a calm and regal face, nailed down and hidden in the earth.

As for Lancelot, he became a hermit in earnest. With seven of his own knights as companions he entered a monastery near Glastonbury, and devoted his life to worship. Arthur, Guenever and Elaine were gone, but his ghostly love remained.

He prayed for all of them twice a day, with all his never-beaten might, and lived in glad austerities apart from man. He even learned to distinguish bird-songs in the woods, and to have time for all the things which had been denied to him by Uncle Dap. He became an excellent gardener, and a reputed saint.

"Ipse," says a mediaeval poem about another old crusader, a great lord like Lancelot in his day, and one who also retired from the world:

Ipse post militiae cursum temporalis,
    Illustratus gratia doni spiritualis,
    Esse Christi cupiens miles specialis,
    In hac domo monachus factus est claustralis.

He, after the bustle of temporal warfare,
    Enlightened with the grace of a spiritual gift,
    Covetous to be the special soldier of Christ,
    In this house was made a cloistered monk.

More than usually placid, gentle and benign,
    As white as a swan on account of his old age,
    Bland and affable and lovable,
    He possessed in himself the grace of the Holy
    Spirit.

For he often frequented Holy Church,
    Joyfully listened to the mysteries of the Mass,
    Proclaimed such praises as he was able,
    And mentally ruminated the heavenly glory.

His gentle and jocose conversation,
    Highly commendable and religious,

Was thus pleasing to the whole fraternity,
Because it was neither stuffy nor squeamish.

Here, as often as he rambled across the cloister,
He bowed from side to side to the monks,
And he saluted with a bob of his head, thus,
The ones whom he loved most intimately.

Hic per claustrum quotiens transiens meavit,
Hinc et hinc ad monachos caput inclinavit,
Et sic nutu capitis eos salutavit,
Quos affectu intimo plurimum amavit.

When his own death-hour came, it was
accompanied by visions in the monastery. The old
abbot dreamed of bells sounding most beautifully,
and of angels, with happy laughter, hauling
Lancelot to Heaven. They found him dead in his
cell, in the act of accomplishing the third and last
of his miracles. For he had died in what was
called the Odour of Sanctity. When saints die,
their bodies fill the room with lovely scent:
perhaps of new hay, or a blossom in the spring, or
of the clean sea-shore.

Ector pronounced his brother's keen, one of
the most touching piece of prose in the language.
He said: "Ah, Lancelot, thou wert head of all
Christian knights. And now I dare say, thou Sir
Lancelot there thou liest, that thou were never
matched of earthly knight's hand. And thou were
the courtliest knight that ever bare shield. And
thou were the truest friend of thy lover that ever
bestrode horse. And thou were the truest lover, of
a sinful man, that ever loved woman. And thou
were the kindest man that ever strake with sword.

And thou were the godliest person that ever came among press of knights. And thou were the meekest man and gentlest that ever ate in hall among ladies. And thou were the sternest knight to thy mortal foe that ever put spear in rest."

The Round Table had been smashed at Salisbury, its few survivors thinning out as the years went by. At last there were only four of them left: Bors the misogynist, Bleoberis, Ector, and Demaris. These old men made a pilgrimage to the Holy Land, for the repose of the souls of all their comrades, and there they died upon a Good Friday for God's sake, the last of the Round Table. Now there are none of them left: only knights of the Bath and of other orders degraded by comparison.

About King Arthur of England, that gentle heart and centre of it all, there remains a mystery to this day. Some think that he and Mordred perished on each other's swords. Robert of Thornton mentions that he was attended by a surgeon of Salerno who found by examination of his wounds that he could never be whole again, so "he said *In manus** boldly on the place where he lay . . . and spake no more." Those who adhere to this account claim that he was buried at Glastonbury, under a stone which said: *HIC JACET ARTURUS REX QUONDAM REX*

---

*"Into Thy hands." The entire phrase, from the death of Jesus (Luke 23:46), is "into Thy hands, I commend my spirit."
†"Here lies Arthur, the Once and Future King."

QUE FUTURUS,† and that his body was
exhumed by Henry II as a counter-blast to Welsh
nationalism—for the Cymry were claiming even
then that the great king had never perished. They
believed that he would come again to lead them,
and they also mendaciously asserted, as usual, his
British nationality. Adam of Domerham tells us,
on the other hand, that the exhumation took
place in April 1278, under Edward I, and that he
himself was a witness to the proceedings; while it
is known that a third search took place in vain
under Edward III—who, by the way, revived the
Round Table in 1344 as a serious order of
knighthood like the Garter. Whatever the real
date may have been, tradition has it that the
bones when exhumed were of gigantic stature, and
Guenever's had golden hair.

Then there is another tale, widely supported,
that our hero was carried away to the Vale of
Affalach by a collection of queens in a magic
boat. These are believed to have ferried him
across the Severn to their own country, there to
heal him of his wounds.

The Italians have got hold of an idea about a
certain Arturo Magno who was translated to
Mount Etna, where he can still be seen
occasionally, they say. Don Quixote the Spaniard,
a very learned gentleman, indeed he went mad on
account of it, maintains that he became a raven—
an assertion which may not seem so wholly
ridiculous to those who have read our little story.
Then there are the Irish, who have muddled him
up with one of the FitzGeralds and declare that he
rides round a rath, with sword upraised, to the

Londonderry Air. The Scots, who have a legend
about

> *Arthur Knyght*
> *Wha raid on nycht*
> *Wi' gilten spur*
> *And candel lycht,*

still swear to him in Edinburgh, where they
believe that he presides from Arthur's Seat. The
Bretons claim to have heard his horn and to have
seen his armour, and they also believe he will
return. A book called *The High History of the
Holy Grail,* which was translated by an irascible
scholar called Dr. Sebastian Evans, says, on the
contrary, that he was safely buried in a house of
religion "that standeth at the head of the Moors
Adventurous." A Miss Jessie L. Eston mentions a
manuscript which she pleases to call *1533,*
supported by *Le Morte d'Arthur,* in which it is
stated that the queen who came to carry him away
was none other than the aged enchantress
Morgan, his half-sister, and that she took him to a
magic island. Dr. Sommer regards the entire
account as absurd. A lot of people called Wolfram
von Eschenbach, Ulrich von Zatzikhoven, Dr.
Wechssler, Professor Zimmer, Mr. Nutt and so
forth, either scout the question wholly, or remain
in learned confusion. Chaucer, Spenser,
Shakespeare, Milton, Wordsworth, Tennyson and
a number of other reliable witnesses agree that he
is still on earth: Milton inclining to the view that
he is underneath it *(Arturumque etiam sub terris*

*bella moventem)** while Tennyson is of the
opinion that he will come again to visit us "like a
modern Gentleman of stateliest port," possibly
like the Prince Consort. Shakespeare's
contribution is to place the beloved Falstaff, at his
death, not in Abraham's, but in Arthur's bosom.

The legends of the common people are
beautiful, strange and positive. Gervase of
Tilbury, writing in 1212, says that, in the woods of
Britain, "the foresters tell that on alternate days,
about noon, or at midnight when the moon is full
and shiny, they often see an array of huntsmen
who, in answer to enquirers, say they are of the
household and fellowship of Arthur." These,
however, were probably real bands of Saxon
poachers, like the followers of Robin Wood, who
had named the gang in honour of the ancient
king. The men of Devon are accustomed to point
out "the chair and oven" of Arthur among the
rocks of their coast. In Somersetshire there are
some villages called East and West Camel (ot),
mentioned by Leland, which are beset with
legends of a king still sitting in a golden crown. It
is to be noted that the river Ivel, whence,
according to Drayton, our "knightly deeds and
brave achievements sprong," is in the same
county. So is South Cadbury, whose rector
reports his parishioners as relating how "folks do
say that in the night of the full moon King Arthur
and his men ride round the hill, and their horses
are shod with silver, and a silver shoe has been

---

*"And Arthur too, stirring wars beneath the earth."

found in the track where they do ride, and when they have ridden round the hill they do stop to water their horses at the wishing well." Finally there is the little village of Bodmin in Cornwall, whose inhabitants are certain that the king inhabits a local tumulus. In 1113 they even assaulted, within the sanctuary, a party of monks from Brittany—an unheard-of thing to do— because they had thrown doubts upon the legend. It has to be admitted that some of these dates scarcely fit in with the thorny subject of Arthurian chronology, and Malory, that great man who is the noblest source of all this history, maintains a discreet reserve.

As for myself, I cannot forget the hedgehog's last farewell, coupled with Quixote's hint about the animals and Milton's subterranean dream. It is little more than a theory, but perhaps the inhabitants of Bodmin will look at their tumulus, and, if it is like an enormous mole-hill with a dark opening in its side, particularly if there are some badger tracks in the vicinity, we can draw our own conclusions. For I am inclined to believe that my beloved Arthur of the future is sitting at this very moment among his learned friends, in the Combination Room of the College of Life, and that they are thinking away in there for all they are worth, about the best means to help our curious species: and I for one hope that some day, when not only England but the World has need of them, and when it is ready to listen to reason, if it ever is, they will issue from their rath in joy and power: and then, perhaps, they will give us happiness in the world once more and chivalry, and the old mediaeval blessing of certain simple people—who tried, at any rate, in their own small way, to still the ancient brutal dream of Attila the Hun.

Explicit liber Regis Quondam, graviter et laboriose scriptus inter annos MDCCCCXXXVI *et* MDCCCCXLII, *nationibus in diro bello certantibus. Hic etiam incipit, si forte in futuro homo superstes pestilenciam possit evadere et opus continuare inceptum, spes Regis Futuri. Ora pro Thoma Malory Equite, discipuloque humili ejus, qui nunc sua sponte libros deponit ut pro specie pugnet.*

Here ends the book of the Onetime King, written with much toil and effort between the years 1936 and 1942, when the nations were striving in fearful warfare. Here also begins—if perchance a man may in future time survive the pestilence and continue the task he has begun—the hope of the Future King. Pray for Thomas Malory, Knight, and his humble disciple, who now voluntarily lays aside his books to fight for his kind.